THE DUKE'S EMBRACE

ERICA RIDLEY

Copyright © 2019 Erica Ridley
Photograph on cover © PeriodImages
Design by Teresa Spreckelmeyer

Never Say Duke

Dukes, Actually

The Duke's Bride

The Duke's Embrace

The Duke's Desire

Dawn With a Duke

One Night With a Duke

Ten Days With a Duke

Forever Your Duke

Gothic Love Stories:

Too Wicked to Kiss

Too Sinful to Deny

Too Tempting to Resist

Too Wanton to Wed

Magic & Mayhem:

Kissed by Magic

Must Love Magic

Smitten by Magic

The *Wicked Dukes Club*:

One Night for Seduction by Erica Ridley

One Night of Surrender by Darcy Burke

One Night of Passion by Erica Ridley

One Night of Scandal by Darcy Burke

One Night to Remember by Erica Ridley

One Night of Temptation by Darcy Burke

CRESSMOUTH GAZETTE

Welcome to Christmas!

Our picturesque village is nestled around Marlowe Castle, high atop the gorgeous mountain we call home. Cressmouth is best known for our year-round Yuletide cheer. Here, we're family.

The legend of our twelve dukes? Absolutely true! But perhaps not always in the way one might expect...

CHAPTER 1

$\mathcal{M}$iss Eve Shelling plastered herself between the smothering red damask of the parlor curtains and the freezing glass panes of the front windows. From the outside, this likely made her look like a madwoman. Eve didn't mind. She wasn't hiding from the outside.

She was hiding from her father.

Eve was also simultaneously keeping an eye out for Wilson, who delivered the afternoon post.

The post was the main reason Eve was avoiding her father. Not their endless rows about rule-following or eternal Christmas or journalistic integrity. She could hold her own on any of *those* topics. But if he caught her intercepting the afternoon post... Or, worse, if he happened to discover what the letters *said*...

Just as her cheek was about to go numb from pressing so hard against the breath-fogged glass, Eve glimpsed Wilson's jaunty green woolen hat heading in her direction.

She slipped out from the curtains, tossed a furtive glance over both shoulders, then cracked open the front door just as Wilson reached the front step.

"Good afternoon, Miss Shelling."

"Good afternoon, Mr. Wilson."

She eased her fingers through the crack just long enough to feel the early winter chill and snatch the thick pile of letters. Eve latched the door as quickly as possible. Father's study might be on the opposite side of the cottage, but he sensed the presence of the slightest draft like a human barometer.

"Damn it, Anderson," Father roared from his office. "You're letting all the warm air out!"

Eve mentally apologized to the very innocent Anderson. As the sole male member of the household staff, Anderson was butler, footman, valet, and anything else that might be needed. At this moment, Anderson was out collecting firewood, but he could return at any time.

All Eve had to do was shove the letters inside her sewing basket and make her way past the open door of her father's study to the privacy of her bedroom without him registering her presence or questioning her motives.

It might have worked, too, if Father hadn't chosen that exact moment to step out of his study with a walking stick in his hand. He was coming her way.

"What are you doing?" he asked suspiciously.

He was always suspicious of her these days. Mostly with good reason.

"Nothing." She tried to look innocent.

There was no time to shove the stack of letters into her sewing basket. Any such movement would only call undue attention to their presence.

It was too late. "Is that the afternoon post?"

"It's for me."

Sort of. She hoped. There hadn't actually been an opportunity to sift through the pile to check names, but if the past four weeks were any indication… every single item would be addressed to the Cressmouth Gazette.

Which was *mostly* her. In spirit, if not legally.

Although her father owned the Gazette, Eve was the one who ran virtually every aspect. It wasn't even unusual for her to handle the correspondence which, historically, consisted of one letter per quarter: The curmudgeonly Duke of Silkridge, begging for his name to be removed from the subscriber list.

Eve didn't think anyone else had even noticed the Gazette, much less bothered to peruse its contents.

Until now.

"*All* of that is the afternoon post?" His eyes widened with obvious incredulity.

Eve gave a weak smile.

No doubt a dozen letters seemed like a proper blizzard of correspondence. Father would be horrified to learn that this was the smallest amount yet. The autumn issue's infamy appeared to finally be dying down.

He clomped forward, placing most of his weight on his walking stick, his eyes nar-

rowed dangerously. "If that's because of that libelous—"

"It wasn't libelous," she interrupted hotly. "Every single word was true."

"—scandalous—"

"Reporting the truth isn't scandalous. That's what real newspapers *do*."

"—foolhardy nonsense you slipped into the paper without my knowledge or consent—"

"Yes," she burst out. "The increased reaction from our readers *is* the direct result of my exposé on our village's founder. Mr. Marlowe was a *man*, not a myth. He was a wonderful visionary and a terrible grandfather to the poor Duke of Silkridge, who—"

"No need to summarize the bloody article. I read it. The whole village read it." He shook the eagle claw of his walking stick at her face. "How many times do I have to tell you that the Cressmouth Gazette only publishes *positive* coverage of *positive* things that happen in our community?"

"It was our biggest seller ever!" Eve flung out her arms in frustration. "We had to go back to press *three times.* Usually issues only go out to people with subscriptions, but this

time locals purchased copies, subscribers ac-tually *read* it—"

"You shouldn't have written it." He pointed at the stack of letters wrinkling in her sweaty hand. "That proves it."

"This?" She lifted the letters high. "Nobody cared about the paper before. This proves I was *right*. Some people speak of Marlowe as though he were the King of England, but others have sent in stories that paint a com-pletely different picture."

Father's gaze was cold. "We don't want to paint a different picture. Our village is known as 'Christmas' and that is the only picture we shall paint. Sleigh rides. Wassailing. Sprigs of holly."

"We write that in every paper." She curled her fingers, every muscle in her body tense. "I'm not suggesting we stop writing about Christmas. I'm suggesting our village is more than *just* Christmas. We could include a selec-tion of reader responses in the opinion columns—"

"The Cressmouth Gazette doesn't *have* an opinion column. We are Christmas. We write about Christmas. That's all our audience wants. The legend of the twelve dukes, casting for *The Winter's Tale*, the latest biscuit flavors

seen in the castle's public buffet. Those are the rules. Follow them."

"Those are your rules," she gritted out. "You invented them; you can change them. I want to be a real journalist who writes real stories."

He grimaced in exasperation. "Why?"

"I want to be taken seriously. I want our paper to be taken seriously. I want our *village* to be taken seriously. Frothy nonsense in a frothy gazette makes people think Cressmouth is nothing but froth, too. We are Christmas and so much more. If we print these opinion essays—"

"We will not."

"Why not? Other newspapers print essays written by constituents." She pinched her lips together, but could not stop the flow of words. "As it stands right now, the Cressmouth Gazette is nothing but a long-winded promotional pamphlet."

"Yes." He slammed the base of his walking stick against the scratched wooden floor. "That is precisely what it is. You do understand. Now go and write about it."

"Don't you think people would find Cressmouth even more interesting if it were presented as a village full of richness and

complexity, rather than a printed stamp whose monochromatic shape never changes, year after year?"

"I think they would stop coming." His lips twisted dismissively. "Tourists don't flock here for stark realism and salacious drama. They come to escape all that. We're not selling mistletoe. We're promising *joy*. The next quarterly printing will be the big annual Yuletide issue."

"The one where we practically include the same word-for-word articles we print every year?"

"Perhaps that is exactly what I should do," he snapped. "The Cressmouth Gazette is an advertisement and a souvenir, nothing more. If you can't adhere to the rules... then you're dismissed."

"You can't give me the sack," she spluttered in disbelief.

"Of course I can. I'm your father and I own the paper."

"I'm your only journalist!"

Eve's fingers clenched around the unread letters clutched in her palm. Father wouldn't *really* run the same articles as last year. Would he?

He sighed. "I know you feel stifled, daugh-

ter. I'm not too proud to compromise. The annual Yuletide issue historically only contains contents related to Yule, but I will allow one uncontroversial, non-Christmas article. This issue, why don't you write about... the swans that live on the castle pond."

"You want me to write two hundred riveting words on aquatic birds located in their natural habitat?" she repeated slowly. "That's a painting, not a story. By the time the paper prints, they'll have migrated south and won't even *be* on the castle pond anymore."

"If it's well received, we can select a different topic for the following quarter." He patted her head and stepped around her to the door. "And if you fail to follow the rules... You won't be *writing* for the paper next year. From now on, every word we print goes through me."

onsieur Sébastien le Duc, known to his family as Bastien and to the rest of the village as the most fashionable man north of London, strolled through the public park adjoining Marlowe Castle, deep in conversation with his elder brother Lucien.

Lucien refused to speak anything but French, which meant most of the passers-by wandering these same paths had little comprehension of the brothers' conversation. This did not bother Bastien in the least. He had not come to a public park to be listened to. He was here to be looked at.

For too many long, unendurable years, he had been forced to stitch every item of his clothing by hand. Just because a gentleman could not afford a tailor was no excuse for slovenly appearance. Bastien had become an expert at little tricks, like only using expensive fabric in areas where it would be seen, and designing garments in such a way as to make them easily alterable to fool the casual eye into believing that one jacket or waistcoat was actually multiple items.

Today, he had not needed to resort to any such tricks. Today, he had money. Today, every single item clinging and sparkling upon his person had been sewn *by someone else* to Bastien's exact specifications.

He felt just as magnificent as he looked.

"Are you even listening to me?" Lucien demanded.

"*Oui*," Bastien answered automatically.

He was not listening. After nine-and-twenty years of brotherhood, Lucien likely knew this. But the only other person who lent half an ear to their brother's stern sermons was their younger sister Désirée, who had just that morning wed a father of two, and now had other things to do with her time.

A flock of whispering, blushing young ladies flitted toward them with a flurry of painted fans and feathered bonnets.

"Good afternoon, Beau," they called out as one, fluttering their eyelashes and flushing prettily.

Bastien preened.

"Oh, for the love of..." Lucien rolled his eyes. "Tell them you shall never be their 'beau.'"

"Let me have this," Bastien reproached him. "Six days a week, I toil in our smithy from dawn to dusk without complaint. Why do you begrudge every harmless flirtation?"

"They're *English*." Lucien shuddered as though the affliction might be contagious. "One cannot trust unmarried young ladies. They all have an ulterior motive."

"Can marriage truly be considered an 'ulterior' motive?" Bastien inquired reasonably.

Besides, his brother was wrong. These ladies wanted a turn in his embrace, not a trip to the altar. He knew that from experience. Although Bastien had not been saving himself for France, the women who gave him the time of day were only interested in sharing a night. It was the sort of "ulterior" motive any self-respecting rake would be honored to indulge.

Lucien sent the ladies his customary all-smiting glower.

They wilted and scurried away.

"You are incorrigible," Bastien informed his brother. "A cad amongst cads. I will find each one of those young women later, and personally make up for your mortifying rudeness."

"At least I won't have to see it." Lucien shrugged. "And soon, you will not have to bother. Now that Uncle Jasper owns his property free and clear, we have nothing tying us to England." His dark eyes shone. "We can finally retake the life we left behind. *Finalement!*"

Bastien could not help but grin. "Returning home to France has been our one overriding aim for so long, I've no idea what I'll do when we get there."

"You'll meet *French* girls," his brother said pointedly.

Bastien brightened. "And shop!"

"And never again step foot in a smithy," Lucien said with a fervent sigh.

A trio of sisters waved as they strolled past. "Good afternoon, Beau!"

Lucien's face turned red. "You are not Beau Brummell. Even Beau Brummell should not be 'Beau' Brummell. He is not French. *We are.*"

"They don't think I'm Beau Brummell," Bastien whispered back. "They think I'm Beau le Duc."

"Even worse," Lucien growled. "Now you will wish to be friends with Prinny."

"What is he saying?" one of the girls asked with curiosity.

Bastien gave them a friendly wave. "That he wishes you ladies a very lovely afternoon."

Lucien's jaw clenched. Although no one but their sister had ever witnessed Lucien attempt to speak a single syllable of English, Bastien had no doubt that his brother understood almost every word.

Not an easy feat. Even after Bastien had become reasonably conversational in English, it had at first been very hard to switch between languages. Now that he was used to doing so all day every day, the right language usually came flying out of his mouth without thinking.

He nudged his brother off the walking path and onto the decorative iron pedestrian bridge that crossed the castle pond. Here, at least, there would be fewer pretty young ladies to vex his brother with their appalling English beauty.

In fact, only one other person stood atop the narrow bridge. Well, two if you counted her dog.

Miss Eve Shelling scowled at the sparkling pond from beneath a drooping straw bonnet. Glossy black tendrils tugged and tumbled with the autumn breeze. Although he could not see her eyes from here, he knew them to be a bright, arresting green, and full of intelligence. Her cloak listed to one side, giving the impression of being tossed over her shoulders more out of habit than respect for fashion, and managed to accentuate, rather than hide, the curves of her silhouette.

At her feet, a large bullmastiff that nearly outweighed her flashed its canines at the swans fluffing their soft white tailfeathers on the water below.

"That is one odd woman," Lucien muttered. "Even for the English."

Bastien *liked* odd. Why else would he have added blue and green spangles to his waistcoat? Odd made life more interesting. He could gaze at Miss Shelling's carelessly beautiful oddness all day.

"This way." Lucien turned away from the bridge.

Bastien glanced over his shoulder at Miss Shelling. "But—"

"That one *definitely* has ulterior motives," Lucien assured him. "And if she has not, her pet certainly does. Do you know why those are called 'gamekeepers' night-dogs?' Because they are strong enough and swift enough to knock armed poachers to the ground, pinning them immobile and helpless until the trespassers can be hanged as a public example."

None of this was making Bastien any less intrigued by Miss Shelling.

"The point is," Lucien continued, as if none of the prior distractions had occurred, "we could leave tomorrow if we wished to. And I think we should."

Of course he did. Much as Lucien would be loath to admit it, when it came to returning to France, Lucien was all emotion and Bastien was the level-headed one plagued by pesky logic.

"We cannot leave tomorrow."

He lifted his hand to give his brother a reassuring pat on his arm, then reconsidered. In Lucien's current mood, he was likely to toss Bastien into the castle pond. This superb greatcoat had been crafted with far too much care to befall such a tragedy.

"Think of Désirée," he tried instead. "She's been married for…" Bastien made a show of checking his pocket watch. "Six and a half hours. Might we grant her a short while to enjoy her new circumstances before we shove her onto a boat?"

"She has lived with him for a month. He's *English*. Surely she must need a break by now," Lucien muttered.

"You *like* Jack," Bastien reminded his brother. "Our percentage of his smuggling operation is the entire reason we were able to pay Uncle Jasper's loan. How much debt do we have now? None. That's thanks to our brother-in-law. Huzzah for Jack! Even though he's English!"

Lucien scowled at him.

Bastien gave him a sunny smile in response. "Now that our finances have broken even, next month we will finally have money left over. We won't just return to France, brother. We'll go home in *style*."

"But when?" Lucien's tortured gaze indicated he'd row across the channel on the back of a fallen log with nary a shilling in his pocket if it would get them home faster.

"After Twelfth Night," Bastien promised. "We cannot split Désirée from her new family over Christmas, no matter how much we'd rather be somewhere else. The sixth of January, we'll set sail for the last time. Can you wait until then?"

Lucien cocked a dark brow. "We will find out."

CHAPTER 3

*E*ve leaned on the cool iron railing of the narrow pedestrian bridge and glowered at the lively pond below.

She liked swans. She just didn't want to waste newspaper space on them.

As if sensing her thoughts, Duenna gave a low growl. Eve stroked behind her bullmastiff's soft ears.

Duenna liked swans, too. Particularly for dinner.

"All right," Eve said. "I'll write about swans if I must, but that's not all I'll write about. There has to be a better compromise. A newsworthy story that might actually interest subscribers without scandalizing Father."

Even if she could think of such a story, things weren't that simple. They never were.

Although he might deny it, Father was still angry with her for inviting an untrustworthy rogue into their home several years before. Not as angry as Eve still was with herself. The consequences had been disastrous. She had sworn to never again fall for a duplicitous blackguard, but promises could not undo the past. Nothing could.

But that didn't stop Father from trying to remake the present. He railed against rule-breakers of any kind, and was determined that the Gazette paint Cressmouth as a real-life fairy story.

The Gazette was just as important to Eve. It was a means to show the world as it truly was—thereby proving there were no hidden tricks to be scared of. That *she* was no longer naïve enough to fall for pretty lies. Only by exposing the truth was anyone ever truly safe.

"There you are!"

Eve glanced over her shoulder and grinned to see her good friend Miss Margaret Church climbing up the iron bridge. "Good afternoon."

"Don't 'good afternoon' me, young lady. I know you're up here plotting something devious, and I insist on taking part."

Because Margaret had already reached her

majority—the ripe old age of five-and-twenty —she considered herself a set-in-her-ways spinster, which she generally used as an excuse to do anything she pleased.

Eve, at the tender age of four-and-twenty, had no such freedoms. There was no inheritance waiting at the end of the rainbow. Her birthday would pass like any other day, and at five-and-sixty she'd probably still be filling her journals with articles that never got published even in the local paper. Assuming her father didn't sack her.

"Good God." Margaret balanced a plump arm on the iron railing. "It cannot be as bad as all that. Did you drop a lemon tart into the water?"

"Worse," Eve said darkly. "Father wants me to write about swans."

Margaret frowned. "As a dining alternative to Christmas pheasant?"

"As… birds who float on this pond for half the year, and then disappear for the other half. They won't even *be* here at Christmas."

"Why, that has nothing to do with Yule at all." Margaret clapped her hands in excitement. "He's unbending! Eve, this is wonderful."

"It's dreadful." She gripped the iron rail.

"Nobody cares about swans that have gone elsewhere. I want to report things that matter. I want to publish real *news*."

"Or, at the very least, not bore people silly. A fine aim. I have just the thing." Margaret struck a dramatic pose. "You can write about me."

Eve pretended to take notes. "Spinster… five-and-twenty… shocking tendency toward self-aggrandizement…"

"Think about it," Margaret insisted. "It could be a regular column. No, not about me every time—more like, 'Cressmouth's resident of the month.'"

"It's a quarterly gazette."

"Then the column will go on forever." Margaret grinned at her. "It's perfect."

Eve scratched behind Duenna's ears and considered the idea. Highlighting a Cressmouth resident every issue was a compromise by Eve's standards, but it would still be a horror to her father. He had despised her column on the village's founder because she'd dared to include less than-rosy aspects of his legacy and personality.

But what if she began by covering the rosiest of residents? Not Margaret. She'd lived on the Continent for a period, which was interesting, but poverty had forced her to leave, which was depressing, and now she lived in a spare room on her cousin's dairy farm, which was… wholesome, Eve supposed. Margaret would gag to think such a saccharine word applied to her.

"I need something bigger," Eve said slowly. "Something Cressmouth-ier."

"A pillar of the community." Margaret nodded. "I understand. The only 'pillars' I let near me are the ones that belong to tall, strapping rogues whose only desire is to—"

Eve covered Duenna's ears. "Please don't say it. She still thinks you're a good influence."

"It's the treats." Margaret fished a crumble of shortbread from her reticule and held it out to Duenna. "Nothing works better than bribery."

The big bullmastiff lowered her muzzle to Margaret's palm and gently retrieved the treat.

"Noelle is very Cressmouth-y," Margaret suggested. "She worked in the castle counting-house for years. Didn't she bake biscuits for the visitors' buffet?"

"'Used to' and 'used to.'" Eve let out a frustrated sigh. She would not be defeated. "I need someone who's the heart of the community at this very moment."

"Do you?" Margaret wrinkled her nose. "I thought you wanted to be a famous journalist, whose name splashes beneath the newsiest news in London. Maybe what you really need is a coach ticket."

"The ultimate aim is London," Eve admitted. "But no writer ever became famous just for buying a coach ticket. If I want anyone to treat a female journalist seriously, first I need experience. If I can turn the Cressmouth Gazette into a real paper, then perhaps I can find employment nearby in Houville or Berwick-upon-Tweed. And once I've proven my competency with that—"

"*Look,*" Margaret breathed, fanning her throat despite the chill autumn air. "It's the le Duc brothers. Has there ever been a more handsome pair? My heart, it's... titillating. Catch me, for I may swoon."

"You won't swoon," Eve pointed out dryly. "You can't gawk shamelessly if your eyes are closed."

"True." Margaret leaned forward on the iron railing. "Sébastien le Duc is almost too gorgeous to look at, but no one can smolder quite like Lucien."

Eve arched a brow. "By 'smolder,' do you mean 'glower broodingly at everything in his path?'"

"*Yes.*" Margaret fanned herself wildly. "I'm definitely going to swoon. Much later. After they walk out of view."

Eve would never admit it, but she'd caught sight of the brothers even before Margaret. They were impossible to miss. Tall, slashing cheekbones and strong jaw due to good blood, well-muscled due to their work in the smithy, dark eyes the color of melted chocolate, a devastating smile that tilted up slightly on one side.

Lucien's hair was so dark it was almost black, full of stray curls that threatened to spill over into his "smolder." His clothes tended to match; black boots, black breeches, black coat, black scowl.

Sébastien, on the other hand, was a burst of color. During the summer months, his perfectly coiffed brown hair lightened to a golden hue. Even during the winter months, he dazzled. Shiny hessians on his feet, tight and buttery buckskins clinging to his muscled legs, a deceptively simple jacket that displayed broad shoulders and narrow hips to best advantage, a snow-white cravat whose impeccable folds defied the winter wind. No matter how hard her heart pounded, she could not look away. Black beaver hat at a rakish angle, strong jaw, and soulful brown eyes. One could not look at him without one's skin heating deliciously.

Eve did not trust either handsome le Duc brother.

She'd learned the hard way that every man kept dark secrets, no matter how pretty his exterior. Or his posterior. They would tell any lie to get what they wanted, and cared nothing about the destruction they left in their wake.

"I shall keep my distance, and I suggest you do the same," she said with a shiver.

"Look-look-look-look-look." Margaret practically wriggled. "Here come the rest of the family."

Sébastien le Duc gamely launched himself into a game of hoop-trundling with his niece and nephew, whilst the newlyweds engaged in an animated conversation with Lucien le Duc.

"That's how I knew his smile matches his brother's," Margaret sighed happily. "It only ever peeks out when he's talking to his sister. That family would do anything for each other."

Eve shook her head. If anything, it looked like Sébastien le Duc was practicing for the circus. He had wrested the toys from his niece and nephew, and was now lurching about the park as he attempted to trundle two hoops at once with both hands.

"Is he *ever* serious?" she said in disbelief.

"Oh, you and your love of serious. I hope you fall for someone who wears his clothes inside out just to vex you."

"I hope you fall for someone who keeps his clothes on, just to vex *you*," Eve shot back.

"Oof." Margaret pantomimed taking an arrow to the heart. "Sooner would I die than live so cruel a fate. So would you, if you had any idea what you were talking about."

"I don't need to know." Eve lifted her chin. If she had no intention of getting married, she had even less inclination to waste precious time with a man she didn't even want to keep around. "I want a career. Until I have it, nothing else deserves my attention."

"Then let's get started." Margaret turned away from the view, her blue eyes serious. "What are we looking at?"

This was what made her such a good friend.

"The 'December' paper is posted on the

first of November, in order to give tourists plenty of time to plan their visit around the annual Yuletide festival. Today is the first Sunday of October. This means I have exactly four weeks to turn the Cressmouth Gazette into something it's not: *newsworthy*."

"Which," Margaret said slowly, "you hope will turn *you* into something you're not."

Eve nodded. "A legitimate journalist. So, here's what I'm thinking…"

They were so engrossed in the branched logistics of what steps to take if Eve's father approved or rejected this or that article, that they did not notice themselves in the path of a runaway iron hoop's trajectory until it clattered against the metal railing right next to them, earning a yelp from Margaret and a disapproving *woof* from Duenna.

Sébastien le Duc flashed them a corsetshedding smile.

"My apologies, ladies. I didn't mean to startle you."

"Or endanger us?" Eve stammered, largely because whenever he was this close, her neatly ordered brain suddenly forgot how to think.

His accent never failed to send prickles of awareness down her spine. Or maybe it was the intensity of those deep brown eyes that pinned her as easily as Duenna could capture a squirrel. Or perhaps it was the knowledge that, no matter how cold the breeze might blow across the water, Eve suddenly felt like she was wearing three layers too many, and that Sébastien le Duc was exactly the sort of man who could help with that type of problem.

"We're busy," she said desperately, scooping the heavy iron ring up from its spot at her feet and shoving it at his perfectly tailored chest. "Good day, Monsieur le Duc."

Shock registered in those come-hither, expressive brown eyes, but he dipped an elegant bow worthy of a king. "A fine afternoon to you as well, ladies."

He took himself off without another word.

Margaret gripped Eve's arm. "Did you just cut him? *You just cut him.*"

"He is a distraction I cannot afford." Eve bit her lip. "And his scent always muddles my brain. He smells... touchable. I don't like it."

Tears of laughter glistened at the edges of Margaret's eyes. "You wanted something newsworthy? This is newsworthy. I'll wager no one has ever turned that gorgeous face away in his entire life."

"Good," Eve muttered. "Maybe he learned something."

"He learned—" Margaret dropped her voice to a dramatic whisper. "—that you intrigue him. The poor man literally just walked straight into a holly bush because he can't stop looking back at you. This is the greatest thing that ever happened in Cressmouth."

"You mean the worst." As amusing as a dandy in a holly bush sounded, Eve couldn't bring herself to look. "The last person I need in my life is some rakish rogue like 'Beau' le Duc."

"Too late." Margaret's eyes sparkled with delight. "He's captivated."

Bastien and Lucien glanced up from their worn family billiards table when their new brother-in-law Jack Skeffington strode into the room.

"I can't believe I'm saying this, but..." Bastien rested his cue. "Shouldn't you be at home with my sister?"

"I should," Jack agreed as he placed an armful of champagne bottles on the tea table in the corner. "And I will."

Lucien gestured. "*Qu'est-ce que c'est?*"

"Veuve Clicquot. Every bottle I have."

Although Lucien posed the question in French, Jack replied in English. Neither had ever budged from this maddeningly stubborn pattern, despite it becoming abundantly clear that they both understood each other's language.

"I'll bite." Bastien crossed his arms over the dove-gray superfine of his favorite coat. "Why are you generously bestowing our tea table with all three bottles of champagne from your enormous wine collection?"

Jack sighed. "Because that's it. For now," he added quickly. "We had a problem at a harbor. Although I sent my best man, both the primary plan and our contingency fell through. He's got the cargo, but the ship is stuck where it is."

"No more champagne?" Lucien leaned against the billiards table for support.

Bastien would do no such thing due to the grievous wrinkles the act of leaning could do to good fabric, but he, too, felt light-headed enough to sit down.

Adding champagne to their brandy smuggling enterprise had allowed them to claw their way out of debt. *Without* the champagne, their brandy commission subsidized what they managed to earn in the smithy, but certainly wasn't enough to finance "going home in style."

It would barely be enough to go home at all.

They needed so much more than sea passage. Transportation once they arrived in France, somewhere to live, something to eat. Little things like that, which Bastien had been planning to cover by saving every spare shilling between now and Twelfth Night.

Except there weren't any shillings. They were debt-free and penniless.

"Don't panic," Jack warned them. "We will resolve this like we eventually resolve everything. But it may take some time."

"Time." Lucien's gaze was empty, his voice dead.

Time was the one thing they simultaneously had too much and not enough of. They'd waited eighteen long years to be able to make their way back home. The idea of waiting an extra week, an extra month, an extra year…

Jack cleared his throat. "That said, I feel it pertinent to mention that we've always known smuggling to be not just a volatile business, but a temporary one. Bonaparte was sent to Elba five months ago. Soldiers are coming home. Taxes and embargoes could lift at any moment, rendering our entire racket unnecessary."

"Thank you," Lucien muttered. "That makes us feel so much better."

"How is Désirée?" Bastien asked hurriedly. "What about your family?"

Jack waved a hand. "We're fine. I have more than enough coin stashed away to ensure my children and grandchildren a comfortable life. I don't need to keep smuggling."

Translation: *So perhaps I won't, even if I still could.*

Bastien nodded. His brother-in-law was right. "Smuggling a temporarily forbidden liquid" inherently was not a life-long career.

Jack had always earned a lion's share of the percentage because he was the brains of the operation as well as its original and on-going financier whenever times were tough.

Bastien and Lucien's involvement was minimal. If anything, Bastien had felt for years that Jack continued to deliver their commission out of friendship more than requiring the brothers' strategic contribution. Before leaving for France, Bastien had planned to tell Jack to keep the entirety of his earnings from now on. He deserved it, and Bastien and Lucien would no longer need it.

Except they did. And it was gone.

"All right," Bastien said before Lucien lost

his mind and started breaking things like a trapped animal. He turned to Jack. "You handle your business, and I'll handle mine. Lucien, do not worry. I have a plan."

Bastien did not have a plan. He had a France-sized ball of nausea roiling in his gut.

"Thank God." Jack's wide shoulders sagged in obvious relief. "I'll resolve this scrape as fast as possible *if* it's possible, but with the current political climate and the way the harbors are managed—"

"We understand," Bastien interrupted. "Our house is not your concern. Go home to your wife. Take her a bottle of champagne."

Jack shook his head. "We have other wines. Those are yours."

He left.

Bastien stared across the billiards table at his brother in dismay. Bastien *wanted* to go home to France. Lucien *needed* to. He was as panicked and desperate as a fish flopping in a bucket, inches from shore.

England was the hook piercing Lucien's skin. He'd brought his siblings here when people were losing their heads at home. The slippery worm of safety was all the bait it took to traipse the trio of siblings out of the only place they had ever known and into nearly two decades of crippling debt, just to own the land beneath their feet.

Bastien gasped. That was it. That was the answer!

Lucien's spine straightened. "You *do* have a plan."

"I do." Bastien raked his fingers through his hair, then cursed himself for messing up a perfectly styled coif. He gestured about the room. "What are you attached to here?"

"Nothing." Lucien curled his lip. "I hate all of it."

Bastien nodded. "For now, the only French things we possess are this carom table, that wine, and our accents. I can change that."

"How?"

"Uncle Jasper deserves the house. He rescued us when we had no safe home to return to. Everything we know about blacksmithing we learned from him, but that was years ago. His gout keeps him out of the smithy. So let's sell it."

Hope lit Lucien's eyes. "We sell the smithy?"

"To the highest bidder." Bastien's heart fluttered with excitement. All they needed was a master blacksmith in want of a fine smithy, and their problems would be solved.

"We'll leave extra coin to Uncle Jasper and take the rest with us to France."

He rubbed the green baize of the billiards table. They didn't need the champagne. They needed a competent, wealthy buyer.

"All right." Lucien handed Bastien his hat. "Go and do it."

Bastien blinked. "Go... walk into the village and sell the smithy to the first rich person who wants it?"

"That is the plan, is it not?" Lucien sank into a chair next to the tea table. "I will wait here. I tend to scare people."

"It's because you're *sullen*," Bastien explained patiently. "It's also the language barrier. I've told you time and again, you catch more flies with—"

"I do not want flies," Lucien interrupted. "I want to go home."

"Twelfth Night," Bastien reminded him. "I promised you, and I keep my word. We have until the sixth of January to complete the sale."

Lucien shook his head. "We don't have until January. We have two months. No one will be working during Christmastide. We need to have the sale drawn up by the first of December and the money in our account thereafter, so that we are ready to go when Twelfth Night comes."

Two months. Surely Bastien could sell a smithy within two entire months.

He put on his hat and strode out the door.

Once he reached the street, he realized he lacked more than a thick winter coat. He needed a plan. "Stroll into the village and sell the smithy" was not a plan.

To Bastien's knowledge, he and Lucien were the only blacksmiths in Cressmouth. That was the only reason their smithy was profitable at all. So who was he supposed to sell it to?

"Good evening, Beau," cooed a chorus of voices from a passing barouche. They didn't slow to speak with him further.

Lucien would say this proved English women weren't worth their time.

Bastien suspected it proved English women felt immigrant blacksmiths weren't worth their time.

It didn't matter. He didn't want an English woman anyway. A night here and there would suffice until they went home. If Lucien was right, if their petition truly managed to reinstate their ancestral lands and status, marriage-minded women would be throwing themselves at their feet. A proper cornucopia of eager French young ladies, all vying to be the next Madame le Duc.

He stopped walking when he reached the castle. Partly because he had no other destination to walk to, and partly because there, standing beneath the drawbridge arch with a journal in one hand and the bullmastiff at her side, was Miss Shelling.

Her carelessly chosen clothes did not make her look disheveled, but rather too busy for the mundane *balivernes* of the ordinary world. Even when she was standing still, Miss Shelling always seemed caught right in the middle of something momentous. She radiated excitement and urgency no matter what she was doing. It was positively magnetic.

She had not noticed him yet. Her glossy black curls were bent over her journal, one hand scribbling furiously as if this was her one chance to commit her thoughts to paper before they vanished into the ether.

Bastien wasn't certain he'd ever had thoughts important enough to write down. He might have been born distantly in line to a title, but he'd spent his adolescence and adult life intimately familiar with long hours of hard work. There wasn't time to scribble thoughts in a smithy. There was just this job, and the next, and the next.

She glanced up and gasped, as if he'd craftily snuck up on her by walking down the middle of the one and only road out of the village to its biggest central landmark.

He made his best leg. "Good evening, Miss Shelling."

She didn't reply *Good evening, Beau*. She stared at him as though no amount of embroidered fabrics and exquisite tailoring could mask what he truly was.

"What do you want?" she asked suspiciously.

He kept a blank face. "I've come to ravish you."

She squeaked and dropped her pencil.

The bullmastiff exposed glossy canines.

"I'm not going to ravish you," he said in exasperation. "I didn't even know you'd be here. You're blocking the entrance to the public castle."

"Oh." A fiery blush covered her cheeks.

Bastien tried not to find it fetching. She was too serious and humorless and clearly felt herself well above Bastien's station, despite only possessing a chaperone of the canine variety. He should just stop talking to her.

She snatched her pencil from the ground and forced herself to meet his gaze. "I've been creeping about Cressmouth since I was little. I dreamed of being a spy when I grew up. My father told me girls couldn't join the army, so I switched paths to journalism." She gave the little book a self-deprecating wiggle. "I still get lost inside my head sometimes. Sorry about that."

Well. That unusual explanation and pretty apology certainly made storming past her in a fit of pique seem like overkill.

He took a step closer.

She didn't move away.

He tried to peek at the journal. "What are you writing about?"

"Swans." Her chin lifted. "And before you say it, I *know* that's the most boring subject in Cressmouth. I'm not doing it for me; I'm doing it for my father. He thinks people want to see pretty things in the Cressmouth Gazette."

"If he wants pretty things…" Bastien hesitated, then forged ahead. "My neighbor likes to sketch. I'm sure she'd be able to create a revoltingly adorable illustration to accompany your fascinating article."

Miss Shelling gazed up at him in wonder. "You're doing me a favor?"

Bastien shrugged. He found solutions. It was a character flaw.

Her eyes narrowed. "In exchange for what?"

Nothing. One performed common acts of kindness out of *kindness*, not self-interest.

Unless one was hoping to spend more time with a certain suspicious, buttoned-up woman.

"A favor in exchange for a favor," he said lightly.

She crossed her arms. "In exchange for what favor?"

He gave her his most untrustworthy smile. "To be determined."

Now *this* was the moment to saunter off on his way, leaving her to stare after *him* in consternation and reluctant fascination.

So he did.

CHAPTER 5

Anything Bastien put his mind to, he mastered.

Learn a baffling new language at the age of ten whilst grieving the loss of his home, his parents, and his childhood? Accomplished. Become a respectable dandy on virtually no budget? Achieved. Take over the village's only smithy when gout prevented his uncle from working? Attained.

Sell said smithy, so that Bastien and his brother could finally return home? Well…

"I am not conceding defeat," he assured Lucien.

"You would never concede defeat." His elder brother seemed amused at such a preposterous idea. "I have just never seen you not make any progress at all. *No* one wants the smithy?"

"It's only been a week," Bastien reminded him. "But, no, I haven't yet found a master blacksmith in the market for an old smithy."

Lucien shook his hand. "We do not require a master blacksmith. We need a buyer. Even some indolent heir who will buy it out of whimsy just to wager it away at the whist table will do fine. All we need is enough money to survive until the courts—"

"No," Bastien said firmly. "*We* can abandon Cressmouth, but we can't abandon *Cressmouth*."

His brother's face twisted in confusion. "What does that mean?"

"It means we're the only blacksmiths! Not just for the villagers, but for all the tourists who come to visit. We are going to sell the smithy, but we'll sell it to someone who can actually run it."

"Who?" Lucien asked, his expression bleak and his voice empty.

"I'm still looking into that," Bastien muttered.

He strode out of the door before his brother could ask more unanswerable questions.

Bastien understood his brother's urgency. Not only had they been desperate to return home ever since they first arrived, but also every moment Bastien spent in the streets trying to sell the smithy, Lucien was alone *in* the smithy. Struggling to communicate with the customers, managing all the jobs by himself, going quietly mad.

Had he believed they had until the first of December to achieve the sale? Lucien would never last that long.

One month, he promised himself. Not a day more. They'd sign the contracts; the banks and the solicitors would take a fortnight or so to do their bit; and then he and Lucien could pack their valises in peace.

But for that to happen, Bastien needed to solve a problem. He didn't know everyone in Cressmouth, and he didn't know anyone outside of it. He needed help to spread the word.

And he knew just the person.

Who was better than a journalist at communicating just the right words to the widest array of people? Luckily for Bastien, Miss Eve Shelling just so happened to owe him a favor.

There was no better time to pay a call than right now.

A spring entered his step as he strolled beneath a canopy of red and orange leaves. The problem wasn't the smithy. The problem was reaching a competent individual who would pay for the privilege of owning it.

The subscribers of the Cressmouth Gazette included persons of means from all over England, whose presence on the distribution list and previous holiday visits indicated how much they loved this village.

If none of the tourists happened to also be master blacksmiths, all was not lost. Wealthy people purchased expensive carriages, whom they would only trust to the hands of the best of the best. Even if they were not themselves blacksmiths, they would *know* one.

It would no doubt tickle their fancy to be able to brag over a fox hunt or an opera box that they were personally responsible for installing their favored smith in the most celebrated Yuletide destination in all of England.

Miss Shelling could sort out the matter with a swish of her pen.

Bastien strolled toward her cottage with his shoulders thrown back and his head held high. Although he had never been invited to her residence, there was no question where it stood. Hers was the only cottage with an outbuilding containing a printing press.

"Good afternoon, Beau," called a pair of her neighbors as he turned the corner onto her lane.

"Good afternoon, ladies," he replied absently, with an automatic tip of his hat.

He was not here to flirt. He was here to—

Miss Shelling flew out of her house with her pelisse untied and her bonnet askew, as if a horde of dragons were hot on her heels. Her bullmastiff shot past her with a growl for good measure.

Bastien took a small step backward just in case.

She dashed between the dwindling cover of two yellow-leaf-shedding birch trees and motioned for him to follow.

After a glance over his shoulder at her innocuous-looking front door, he joined her between the trees, careful not to let the spindly branches scrape the ivy-green superfine of his best jacket.

"Were you just going to walk up to my front door?" she hissed before he could ask what on earth had sent her into such a panic.

Ah. The answer was: him. Boldly strolling down a public street during the hours most common for paying an afternoon call.

Unsolicited.

"Yes," he replied. There was no point in prevaricating.

She took a deep breath. "Don't. Please."

Bastien had the distinct impression that he was not only "not good enough" for Miss Shelling, she couldn't even bear the thought of being seen with him.

"I am not here to make romantic overtures," he said icily. "I am here because you owe me a favor."

The storm of emotions that crossed her pretty face might have been humorous in some other context.

"This way." She took off through what was definitely not a walking path, paying absolutely no attention to the dirt beneath her boots or the russet-and-gold leaves that crumbled against her pelisse as she barreled through the trees.

Jaw clenched, Bastien picked his way behind her as swiftly and as carefully as he could.

She might not care if she emerged on the other side with more twigs than hair and a pelisse riddled with leaves, but Bastien literally could not afford to repair a ruined coat, even if he made the alterations himself.

"Here." She burst through the trees and

pointed at a small outbuilding. "That's where we print the Gazette. If you *must* speak to me privately, we can do so in there. That's where I spend most days anyway. It's accessible from the back, so you needn't ever come to the front."

Never show his face near her door. Message received. He brushed the leaf dust from his hat.

"I don't know what sort of favor you think I came to ask, but I assure you, it is no secret. The opposite. My brother and I are selling our smithy, and I was hoping you could help us spread the word to the right people."

She stared at him for a long moment without blinking.

Why? Was she thrilled to see the last of him? Annoyed he'd come to collect on the favor? Worried who would forge iron replacement pieces to the printing press once he and Lucien were no longer here?

He matched her unblinking stare with his own. And then blinked. *Damn* it.

"Are you leaving or just selling?" she asked at last.

He smiled politely. "Are my personal plans subsequent to the sale relevant?"

"No," she admitted. "I ask questions. Old habit."

Bastien doubted it was habit, and more like strategy. Not an ulterior motive, but a blatant one. She was a journalist. It was her job to ask, even if she was uninterested in the subject. Just like the swans.

"Yes," he said. "We're returning to France."

Alarm filled her eyes. "All of you? What about—"

"Just Lucien and I. Désirée's home is now here."

At this, her searching gaze clouded with even more questions, and she visibly forced herself to push them away.

"I'll help." She retrieved a pencil and a journal from inside her pelisse. "What do you have in mind?"

"Nothing concrete," he admitted. "I've spoken to everyone I know here in the village. You know people all over England. I'd like to reach them."

Her face lit up and she began to scribble. "An advert. You want to place an advert in the next Gazette."

He frowned. "The Gazette doesn't have an advertisement section."

"It does now." She lifted her eyes from the journal and met his gaze. "A favor for a favor, yes? Father adores the illustration your friend made of the swans. I can convince him to run this."

"Easily?" If this advertisement didn't print, Bastien would be right where he was now: nowhere.

She bit the end of her pencil. "Father doesn't want the Gazette to become 'focused on profit,' but he *does* want Cressmouth to keep fulfilling the idyllic dream. He'd rather run an advert than risk visitors not coming because we no longer meet their needs. What would you like the advert to say?"

"I was hoping you could help with that, too."

Because he'd studied obsessively for years and spent six days a week speaking to apprentices and customers from dawn to dusk, Bastien's command of English was superior to both his siblings'. That did not make him a writer. He could flirt with ladies and discuss ideal wheel circumferences at length, but he didn't know how to pick the right words to convince someone to purchase a smithy in the northernmost corner of England.

"Mm-hmm." She was scribbling again, as if just the right phrasing constantly flowed from her pencil tip and all she needed to do was set it to paper.

Bastien shut his mouth and waited.

He should not find her fetching. She'd rather scurry amongst the trees like a squirrel than be seen in his presence. Her bonnet still lurched to one side, leaving a spill of ebony curls to tangle in the cold breeze. Her pelisse gaped at her hips, revealing a sliver of ink-stained apron.

This was not the sort of woman one had *fun* with. She was the marrying type, the bet-ter-than-you type, the all-business-no-plea-sure type. The stay far, far away type.

And yet. Whatever she was scribbling put a seductive sparkle into her green eyes. Her pink lips plumped perfectly every time she nibbled the edge of her pencil. The relentless wind brought a becoming blush to her cheeks. And she was standing out here at the edge of the winter woods, doing her best to help him leave for good.

He cleared his throat. "Miss Shelling..."

"Eve," she said without looking up. "If we're doing favors for each other, you might as well call me Eve."

Bastien blinked. What was he meant to do with *that?* He was at liberty to use her Christian name at will, but forbidden to knock upon her door?

"Sébastien," he said, for there could be no other gentlemanly reply. "Friends call me Bastien."

There. Either she would say *we shall never be friends,* or she'd be forced to murmur *you should come for tea sometime.*

She did neither.

"I've got it!" Miss—er, *Eve*—spun her journal around to face him. "This is perfect. The Gazette subscribers refer to themselves as the 'friends of Christmas' and include almost everyone who has ever visited, as well as a great deal of their friends. Our village's permanent residents might number in the hundreds, but the Gazette reaches thousands."

Thousands? Bastien's chest lightened. This was going to work. He could feel it.

"Well?" she prompted. "What do you think?"

"I think," he said slowly, "that this is a much larger favor than the one I did for you."

"Don't worry." She nibbled the edge of her pencil, her eyes sparkling. "It is your turn to be indebted to me."

He choked on a startled laugh. "Fair enough. When will the advertisement go out?"

"Publication is intended for the first of November. I set the type and run the press a week in advance so that we can start shipping to the furthest places first. We cannot guarantee everyone will receive their copy on the same day, but we try."

"Impressive," Bastien said, and meant it.

It was also only three weeks away. Lucien might find such a timetable interminable, but this was the best chance they had. Someone would know someone. The smithy would be sold before they knew it. In fact, as soon as Bastien returned home, he would send away for tickets to book their passage to France. That would make it seem final, and give them both something to hold onto.

He tipped his hat to Eve. "Thank you."

She pointed her pencil toward a break in the trees on the opposite side of the outbuilding. "That way to the main road. There's a walking path."

Thank God. This jacket had to last until the Gazette found them a buyer.

He set off with his chest much lighter than

it had been in years. Whatever Eve wanted as her return favor, she'd have to hurry and ask for it.

After Twelfth Night, Bastien and his brother would be gone.

CHAPTER 6

*E*ve spread new sheets of foolscap over the large wooden table next to the printing press.

Three weeks from now, this table—and every inch of the floor around it—would be piled high with the December issue of the Cressmouth Gazette. The Yuletide edition was the biggest of the year. A fortnight from now, printing would begin.

As the sole typesetter, the entire writing staff, and one half of the printing team, this meant time was running out for Eve to finalize the contents and layout in time for her father's approval. A smile curved her lips as she imagined garnering his favorable opinion at last.

Bastien le Duc might think that her ability

to help his message reach thousands of people made her contribution the bigger favor, but he had helped her reconcile with the one person she cared about most.

Father had viewed the swan illustration as exactly what it was: an olive branch. He would still scrutinize every single square of type before they went to press, but between now and then she had her autonomy again... *and* the old, easygoing father-daughter relationship she'd missed.

Duenna's nose nudged Eve's feet beneath the table.

"Not yet." Eve scratched behind Duenna's ears. "We'll go for a walk later."

Duenna cast her a mournful gaze, then rested her muzzle atop Eve's foot as though to say, *Feeling trapped? Perhaps a brisk stroll would do the trick. Shall we see?*

"Soon," Eve promised.

Drafting a quarterly gazette wasn't nearly as intensive as she imagined producing a daily newspaper would be. For that reason, Eve wanted each issue to shine.

Her father might be content with rerunning old articles extolling Castle Marlowe's vast accommodations, the free communal dining area open to tourists and locals alike, and the countless seasonal activities ranging from sleigh rides to caroling to performances of *The Winter's Tale.*

To Eve, Cressmouth might be known as "Christmas" but that wasn't *all* it was. Every wassailer and mistletoe grower and fruitcake vendor was a vital part of a rich, complex community. The trick was finding a way to announce that message to the world.

Margaret's suggestion of Resident of the Month wasn't a bad idea, but with an entire village of hardworking, worthy neighbors to choose from, how was Eve supposed to decide—

She dropped her pencil. "The smithy!"

Duenna jerked her head up and let out a plaintive howl.

"No, I don't mean we're going there right now." Eve grabbed her bonnet from the table. "Actually, yes. That's exactly what I mean. Are you ready? Who wants to go for a walk?"

Duenna woofed and leapt upright.

"This will work brilliantly," Eve informed her lively bullmastiff as they hurried from the printing house.

She'd write about what an intrinsic part of the community the smithy was. Everyone entered Cressmouth on the same winding road, making the smithy the first business visitors saw as they reached the village. It was where carriages were mended, iron hoops were crafted, replacement parts were forged.

This time of year, sleighs often queued around the smithy for annual maintenance. If she could procure an illustration depicting *that*, Father couldn't have any objections to the relevance of the article. Eve would help Bastien sell his smithy, prove Cressmouth was more than a holiday, and prove herself and her gazette as more than just froth.

Who knew? If she continued in this direction, perhaps by next Christmas she'd be a respected journalist at an even bigger publication.

Eve drew to a stop as she and Duenna reached the edge of the le Duc property. The family residence was nestled back toward the evergreens, but the smithy was right next to the main road. The large doors were wide open, exposing the flurry of activity inside.

Now that she was here, Eve hesitated. Wanting to be a respected journalist of meaningful articles was one thing. Barging into someone's place of business with a pencil and a bullmastiff was another.

She wouldn't barge, Eve decided. She

would enter quietly and keep to the back. Assuming there was a back. Having never actually *been* in the smithy—her family had no carriage to maintain, and Father always handled replacing machinery himself—Eve was belatedly realizing she had absolutely no idea how a smithy worked.

Well, that was why she was here, wasn't it? To investigate, and to report. She'd wager a fair percentage of the Gazette's wealthy subscribers were also unfamiliar with the inner workings of a smithy. Her article would educate as well as entertain.

She strode in through the front door.

No one scurried out of sight, or rushed to hide objects from view. Eve didn't *expect* such things, but she'd also come to learn that the people with the most to hide usually were the same people one least suspected.

Now that she was here and everything seemed normal, she could finally admit to herself how badly she'd been hoping that was true. She *liked* Bastien. She *wanted* to write this article. And it wouldn't happen if her father found any reason at all to blackball it.

She glanced around for a bench or chair. The only visible stools were currently in use, as a lad stood atop one to adjust a... something, and another lad leaned on his as he adjusted… something else.

This wasn't going to be a *technical* article, Eve decided quickly. She wasn't trying to explain how to be a blacksmith. She just needed to convey the importance of the smithy's location and function within the community. And relate it to Christmas, of course.

"Just a little froth," she muttered to herself. "Mostly serious, lightly frothy."

"Eve?"

She spun around to find herself face-to-face with Bastien le Duc, as she'd never seen him before.

Gone were the outrageous colors, the pristine cravat, the impossible dandy perfection. Instead, white linen sleeves rolled up to his elbows, revealing calloused fingers and unfashionably bronzed forearms. A nondescript tunic replaced his usual eye-catching waistcoat. Now what caught the eye were his strong shoulders, his well-muscled body, the throat-drying way his tousled dark hair clung to his brow.

She gulped. "I…"

Didn't know you could look even more attractive than you normally do.

He tilted his head. "Is this about the advert?"

"Yes. No." Why was she here again? She took a deep breath. "I want to write an article about the smithy."

A blur of melodic French shot out from beneath a carriage.

Bastien responded in kind, without taking his eyes off Eve.

Scuffed black boots swung out from under the carriage, followed by worn buckskins, an indecently exposed white linen shirt, and the eternally broody eyes of Lucien le Duc.

Margaret would melt into a puddle if she could see him now.

Eve kept her gaze locked on Bastien. One gorgeous, rumpled, well-muscled le Duc brother was more than enough distraction.

"It's not some sort of exposé," she said hurriedly. "If that's what your brother is worried about." At least, she didn't think it was. For years she'd relied on her belief that everyone had something to hide, but she'd never wanted to be more wrong than right now. "I think it will help the advert if I can explain how important this smithy is to the community." She glanced at the rows of waiting carriages. "And how popular."

Lucien let fly with another stream of euphonic French, smirked, and then disappeared between two carriages.

Bastien cleared his throat. "He says 'popular' doesn't pay the accounts and I shouldn't waste time talking to you."

She frowned. "Wait… Lucien understands English? Then why does he—"

"Here." Bastien swung his brother's abandoned stool in her direction. "Have a seat. I won't try to decipher Lucien, but I can explain what he was referring to. Most of our jobs are paid."

She paused in the act of retrieving her journal and pencil. "Most?"

"Our scale depends on need." He shrugged. "If you can afford our regular rates, you pay them. If you cannot, we negotiate. Sometimes that means accepting lower rates. And sometimes that means accepting IOUs in lieu of payment."

"And sometimes *that* means you never do get paid." She flipped open her journal. "I'm writing this down."

"Don't." Bastien pulled a face. "I doubt 'occasionally operates at a loss' is much of a selling point for the advert."

Eve stopped writing mid-word.

"Probably not," she admitted. But it spoke very highly of the le Duc character. "I'll stick with 'well-respected' and 'popular.'"

"I can't take any of the credit." He fished a rag from his leather belt and started wiping the carriage his brother had been working on. "Our Uncle Jasper founded this smithy before any of us were born. He slept abovestairs in the attic until…"

She glanced up, her pencil poised. "Until?"

"Until he suddenly had a family to house." He disappeared beneath the carriage as if to say, *Conversation over.*

Eve was far from done, however. She was starting to suspect that the men who ran the smithy were just as intrinsic to the community as the smithy itself.

They could sell the building to the highest bidder, but what sort of blacksmith would take their place? Someone who would sleep in a crawlspace to keep his prices low for locals? Or someone who would match his prices to the purses of the fancy London tourists, making it all but impossible for anyone who actually *earned* their money to be able to afford the smithy's services?

The le Ducs needed a buyer. Cressmouth needed the *right* buyer. Someone who cared about the community as deeply as he cared about profits.

This might well be the most important article Eve had written in her entire career.

With Duenna settled comfortably beside the stool, Eve turned to a blank page and began to record everything she witnessed happening around her.

It was impossible to know which of the brothers was the more skilled blacksmith, but Bastien was the one who was constantly interrupted by everyone who entered the smithy. He took orders, assigned jobs, exchanged banking information or accepted IOUs, explained repairs, cautioned about upkeep, assigned carriages to stalls, determined the order of operations, manually inspected the forge.

All of this, whilst seamlessly translating running commentary between his brother and the customers, or the lads Bastien referred to as "apprentices."

Eve knew next to nothing about smithies, but she doubted these lads were old enough to be true apprentices. Were there no journeymen in Cressmouth? She made a note to investigate both here and in the neighboring towns.

Providing work to local adolescents who undoubtedly needed the coin was a commendable gesture, but also not likely to make the smithy's purchase more attractive to potential buyers... Though it did make Bastien even more attractive to Eve.

He and his brother made quick work of their tasks, despite pausing as many times as necessary to answer client questions or patiently show their apprentices how to make this adjustment or use that tool.

Meanwhile, the brothers tossed what Eve could only assume to be jokes and insults back and forth, based on their tone of voice. Every now and then, one or the other would make an offended expression and then burst into laughter, the wickedness in their matching smiles lighting up the room and everyone in it.

"Stop staring," she muttered to herself.

Bastien le Duc turning out to be talented and kindhearted and responsible and patient and funny instead of just a ridiculously good-looking dandy didn't signify in the least.

He was *leaving*. She was helping him go. Nothing mattered but Cressmouth and the Gazette.

"Teatime," Bastien shouted.

Eve glanced around. There was no tea.

The lads streamed out the open doors.

"Where are they going?" she asked.

"Home to tea." He dragged a stool next to her and sat with his head leaning back against the wall. "Or to take a nap. Afternoon break is a half-hour. I definitely needed mine." He pretended to snore.

She thwacked his knee with her notebook just as Lucien walked past and shot her a ferocious scowl.

He didn't fool Eve. She'd seen him chuckle. But she glared right back out of solidarity.

"So..." She turned back to Bastien. "There's no tea?"

"None," he confirmed without opening his eyes. "Come back after we've sold the smithy."

She bit her lip and let herself gaze at him for a moment. His eyes were closed and no one but Duenna was there to witness her doing so for as long as she pleased.

Bastien was pretending to be exhausted probably because he truly *was* exhausted, but didn't want her thinking so. The rugged, irresistibly tousled blacksmith he was right now looked nothing like the perfectly coiffed, fresh-shaven dandy he presented himself as whenever he wasn't in the smithy.

Which was the real man?

"Are you looking forward to selling the smithy?" she asked softly.

It was not the same question as, *Do you want to sell the smithy?* That answer was yes. Eve didn't doubt him. But she knew from experience that one could want a thing and dread its inevitability at the same time.

At first, she thought he wouldn't answer. Perhaps he really had fallen asleep. Or perhaps her question was too personal.

Then he opened his eyes. "I look forward to returning to France."

Ah. So he did know what it was like to want a thing and not want it at the same time. Between the two choices, France would always win. But that didn't mean he wouldn't miss some of the things he left behind.

She gave him a half-smile. "You like Cressmouth."

"Do I?" He affected indignation. "Maybe I like breaking my back whilst covered in oil, sweat, and blisters."

Her smile grew wider. "You like the smithy, too."

She expected him to prevaricate. Instead,

he shrugged and gave her a sheepish grin. "Right on both counts. Don't put it in the paper."

Eve pretended to cross out her notes. "The article is much shorter now."

"The advert was a good favor." His brown eyes held hers "But a feature article feels like more than I can afford to pay you ."

"You're not paying me," she said quickly. "This is a mutual favor. I swear my motives are more selfish than philanthropic."

"Mine, too." He frowned. "You still deserve to be paid for your work."

"Don't *you?*" She pointed at all the projects and carriages waiting for his attention.

His dimple flashed and he pushed to his feet. "Break's over. Have to get back to my post before the lads think everyone can sit down anytime they like."

Just as she opened her mouth to ask *What lads?*, they came streaming back through the open door, laughing and snapping threadbare rags at each other's shoulders.

Lucien stalked back in, but didn't bother to glare at her. He just went straight to work before the roaring hot forge.

"See that?" she whispered to Duenna. "We're positively growing on him."

But the truth was, Bastien was the one growing on Eve.

She couldn't get him out of her mind as she led Duenna out of the smithy and back up the winding road toward the printing house.

Perhaps it was because he had been honest with her, even when it did not serve his best interest. Perhaps it was because he had let her see him at what he likely believed to be his worst. Perhaps it was because he had accepted her decision to write about his smithy without question or argument.

Perhaps it was because they had been alone together for twenty-nine minutes and he had made no attempt to press unwelcome rakish advances upon her.

Unwelcome was a strong word. A false word. An outright, barefaced lie.

If he'd bothered to try, she would have grabbed hold of that tattered tunic and kissed him until she forgot her own name.

CHAPTER 7

*E*ve stepped back from the interior stone wall of the castle vestibule to admire her handiwork.

Most visitors passed through this entranceway. Marlowe Castle wasn't just Cressmouth's largest and most iconic landmark, it was their lodging-house, their pub, their assembly rooms, free meals thrice daily in the common rooms. Every *local* passed through this entranceway multiple times per month, if not every day.

And now it contained a community posting wall for signs and bills. Eve had secured permission from Mr. Thompson, the castle solicitor. Since she was the first to know about it and therefore the first to use it, the community posting wall was currently one hundred percent covered in identical bills she'd printed by the dozens to advertise the sale of the le Duc smithy.

Reaching thousands of wealthy patrons was one thing. Finding someone as competent and caring as the le Duc brothers was quite another. If the entire village worked together, perhaps they could perform their own Christmas miracle.

Satisfied for now, she exited the castle and headed back toward the printing house with Duenna prancing right beside her.

Only a fortnight remained before the Yuletide issue went to print. Not a moment could be wasted.

Outside, the crisp autumn day had turned gray with thunderclouds. A freezing wet raindrop hit the middle of her forehead and slid down the side of her nose. She'd worn her pelisse, but had no umbrella. If the heavens opened, she was going to get soaked.

Head down, Eve sprinted down the main road and took the shortcut through the trees to use the leaves as cover. When she burst through the other side, she came to an immediate standstill.

Bastien le Duc was standing beneath the branches of an apple tree beside the printing house, impeccably dressed in touchable soft gray superfine, the brim of his beaver hat pulled low to shield his eyes from the occasional drop of rain.

His face lit up when he saw her.

Eve's heart flip-flopped in response. She forgot about the printing house and walked to him instead.

"What are you doing here?"

He stared back at her, his gaze inscrutable. "The smithy is closed on Sundays."

"So you thought you'd spend your one free day here in my garden?"

"I never said I intended to be here all day." His eyes dropped to her mouth. Her throat went dry. "Is that what you want?"

It was definitely what she wanted.

To give her hands something to do other than reach for him—and to occupy her mouth with something safer than begging for kisses—she plucked an apple from the tree and took a bite out of pure self-preservation.

"Teatime?" he asked politely.

Eve nodded. She would stay three paces away and gnaw every apple on this tree like a one-woman flock of squirrels if that was what it took to keep from complicating a friendship that was doomed from the beginning.

He took a step closer.

She yanked an apple from the tree and all but chucked it at his waistcoat.

He caught it one-handed and shined the rosy flesh on the ivy superfine of his greatcoat. "Thanks."

There. Now they were both busy with apples. All they could do was talk.

"Why didn't you go home sooner?" she asked.

A flicker of confusion crossed his face.

Blast. She hadn't meant it like that.

"Not that I wish you would have," she babbled quickly. "It's just, if you've been dying to return to France, and nothing stopped you from going there other than selling off the smithy—"

"Nothing else is stopping me *now*," he corrected. "Uncle Jasper was leasing the smithy. After he brought the three of us here, he needed somewhere to put us. He made an agreement with Mr. Marlowe for the land you probably think of as 'the le Duc farm.'"

Eve froze in alarm. The article she'd written about their mercurial founder hadn't included everything she'd uncovered about his sometimes capricious way of "helping" people.

Her stomach twisted. "Not a good arrangement?"

"Not a good arrangement," Bastien confirmed grimly. "But the best arrangement we had. The *only* arrangement. Repay Mr. Marlowe's quoted price with interest within twenty years, or have every inch of the land beneath our feet revert to the castle's ownership overnight."

She winced. "And you did it?"

"We did it." He thrust his shoulders back, his brown eyes gleaming with pride. "As of a fortnight ago, the le Duc family is debt free, and Uncle Jasper owns that farm outright."

"That's wonderful," Eve said, and meant it.

Or maybe she meant *he* was wonderful. Staying in a place he longed to leave, working his fingers to the bone, in order to pay off land he didn't intend to live on or ever see again, just to make sure his uncle's future was secure.

"Don't put it in the paper." He gave a self-deprecating smile.

She shook her head. "I wasn't thinking about the paper."

He took a step closer. "What were you thinking about?"

Where was his apple? Where was *her*

apple? Somehow she'd eaten it, stem and all, or else it had fallen unnoticed from her fingers, because right now there was nothing at all in her hands. They were perfectly free to reach for his lapel, or slide their way up his shoulders to where his hair curled against the back of his cravat.

Bastien's eyes didn't leave hers. "It's raining harder."

Was it? She stepped closer. "I don't mind."

The tips of their boots grazed.

"I should warn you," he said, his voice husky. "I *am* leaving. Nothing can come of any mutual attraction between us. In fact, I have tried very, very hard to banish you from my mind."

Her breath and his heartbeat tangled together. "Did it work?"

The corner of his mouth quirked up. "I'm here, aren't I?"

"Not close enough," she whispered.

He cupped her face in his hands and slanted his mouth over hers.

She felt his kiss everywhere. Her heart clanged, her toes curled, her flesh tingled. Had she thought the day cold? The heat of his mouth stoked a fire in her core. She wouldn't be surprised if every raindrop evaporated into puffs of steam around them.

Boldly, she ran her palms up the hard muscles of his arms as she'd dreamed of doing, then plunged her fingers into his hair.

His hat lurched askew, then tumbled off his head entirely. Bastien didn't reach for it. Instead, he reached for *her*, spanning his hands on the curve of her hips, pulling her close.

The thunder roaring above them barely masked the clanging of her heart. She pressed herself against him, wet bosom to wet chest, and returned each kiss with a wantonness she hadn't known she possessed.

He tasted tart and sweet like the apple, but also as dark and forbidden as he'd warned her. Perhaps that was why she'd thrown caution to the wind. Kissing him was safe. It didn't mean anything. He couldn't disappoint her. He was *leaving*. This wasn't romance. This was elementary. Iron, smelting in a forge. Lightning, streaking across the sky. Thunder—

No, not thunder. That growl belonged to—

"Duenna, *no!*" was all Eve managed to gasp before her overprotective bullmastiff launched her full eight stone of solid muscle into the man she believed to be mauling her owner.

Because they happened to be locked in an embrace, Eve splashed into the rain puddle right with him.

His shocked eyes met hers. "Was that an elephant?"

"Close." Their noses brushed. "Bullmastiff."

"Will she do it again if I try to rescue you?"

She pushed a hunk of wet hair from her eyes. "Let's find out."

"Come on." Eyes sparkling, he pulled her to her feet and raced with her through the driving rain to the printing house's awning.

As soon as they tumbled through the doorway, Eve shut the door firmly behind them.

Duenna howled her displeasure from the other side.

"You likely gave us pneumonia!" Eve shouted against the sound of the rain.

"Now we're giving it back," Bastien added.

They looked at each other and burst out laughing.

"This way." Eve led him to a small fireplace at the rear of the one-room outbuilding. "I never light this when we're printing, but I think 'soaked to the skin' counts as a valid reason."

"It's an excellent excuse for a lot of things," Bastien agreed, his quick gaze taking in the room about them. "Or it would be, if there was furniture."

She widened her eyes. "There's a very lovely printing press."

"Not what I was thinking." He flashed her an unrepentant grin. "And probably for the best."

Eve shrugged out of her wet pelisse and hung it by the fire, then placed her boots before the grate to dry.

Following her lead, Bastien pulled off his boots and placed them next to hers, then hung his sopping coat and waistcoat on the opposite side of the fire. His linen shirt was all but transparent in the firelight, revealing every muscle of his chest. She swallowed hard.

His intense gaze met hers. "Now what?"

"Now…" She tugged the sole rug before the fire and pulled him close to join her. "We keep our cold toes on this warm carpet until our clothes are dry and the rain has stopped."

He wiggled his brows. "Let me make sure I understand the rules. As long as we keep our feet on this two-foot-square scrap of carpet, we can do anything we wish?"

"And stay vertical," she added. "Anything we wish whilst also vertical."

His eyes sparkled. "That... doesn't limit things quite as much as you seem to think."

Her face flushed hot. He was right; she had no idea how much wickedness one might enjoy whilst standing upright before a fire. Until him, she'd never wanted to find out.

"Kissing," she blurted desperately. "I'm asking you to kiss me."

But as he enveloped her in the heat of his embrace, she couldn't help but suspect that before long, she'd be begging for much, much more.

CHAPTER 8

Bastien poked his head into his brother's open doorway. "Ready?"

Even before Lucien lifted his dark gaze, it was clear that, no, Lucien was not ready. Well, not for their usual wind-in-their-hair, hell-for-leather dash through the woods in their beloved racing phaeton.

Lucien was on his knees in the center of the room, wiping down a battered leather valise with a clean rag.

"*Non*," he answered. "I'm packing."

Bastien shifted his feet. "I haven't sold the smithy yet."

"If you have faith in Miss Shelling and her newspaper, then so do I. But more important-ly…" Lucien's eyes met Bastien's. "I have faith in *you*. If you swear we will be on a boat by

Epiphany, then we will be on a boat by Epiphany."

Normally, such a statement of unconditional confidence from his brother would have filled Bastien with pride. Or, at least, a frisson of excitement at the thought of their upcoming journey home.

Today, something restless deep inside him needed that wild, reckless ride in an open phaeton all the more.

"I'll be back in an hour," he told his brother.

Lucien didn't even look up. The valise before him might still be empty, but clearly Lucien's mind was already eight hundred miles away.

Bastien had already readied the horses and carriage. All that remained was to leap up onto the waiting bench and take the reins. Without Lucien, the carriage would be lighter; the horses even faster.

But without his brother, the seat beside him just felt… empty.

Dawn was still breaking. Their favorite time to fly through the village. No one in the street, and a beautiful sky all around them.

He gave the horses their heads, as he always

did. The phaeton was the one thing in their lives that made them feel free. Soon, they wouldn't need to pretend. They'd be back home in France, untethered from England forever.

Bastien concentrated on the wind unraveling his cravat and rumpling his hair to keep himself from identifying the strange emptiness hiding deep within his chest.

The streets weren't completely empty. A woman in the distance was out walking her dog.

Not just any dog. A bullmastiff.

He slowed, the emptiness in his chest forgotten. How many times must he and Lucien have flown past Eve and her dog in the wee hours of the morning? Hundreds? Thousands?

They'd never once slowed. Her presence was just another pretty component of Cressmouth's picturesque background, like snowcapped evergreens or mistletoe growing on oak trees. Except oak trees had never made his heart beat faster.

He pulled up beside her. "Good morning, Duenna."

Eve's face jerked up toward his, her mouth wide with faux offense. "And me?"

"Oh, you too, Eve." He grinned at her. "I didn't see you there."

She pointed at his chest. "Now, Duenna. Attack!"

Duenna sniffed beneath her tail.

"Maybe I have to be kissing you for that to work," he suggested, making a wide-eyed, earnest expression. "Should we try it?"

The glances she sent over her shoulders were almost comically horrified. "*Shh.* Someone might hear you."

Comical, perhaps, if he hadn't spent the entire night dreaming of pulling her into his embrace again.

He patted the empty seat next to him. "Come on up."

She narrowed her eyes. "Are you summoning me like a dog?"

"Oh, Eve, you're still here. Of course, you can come, too. Don't you agree, Duenna?"

Duenna leapt into the open phaeton and flopped at Bastien's feet.

"Traitor," Eve muttered.

Bastien held out his hand. He'd leap down to help her in like a gentleman, but there was nowhere to tie his horses. They would have to do it this way, together.

She grasped his hand. He pulled her up

and into the carriage. She settled beside him with a roll of her eyes.

He grinned. The seat wasn't empty anymore. It looked perfect.

She arched an eyebrow. "Who are you racing today?"

"No one. We're not professional racers," he explained. "We dash around at breakneck speed at five o'clock in the morning down the side of a mountain just for sport."

"*Men*," she grumbled, with a haughty sniff. Her twinkling eyes gave her away.

All the same, he settled the horses into a sedate rhythm, letting the phaeton amble along the winding road with all the haste of a tortoise.

Duenna placed her paws atop Eve's lap in order to gaze over the sidewall with her tongue lolling from her mouth.

Bastien stuck out his tongue and pretended to do the same thing.

Eve smacked his leg. "Don't mock my dog, or I'll besmirch your character in the article I'm writing."

"I wasn't mocking her," he protested. "I was aspiring to *be* her. Feel free to put that in the paper. I'd wager lots of people wish they were dogs."

She pulled out her journal and made a note.

He scratched behind Duenna's ears. "How is it going?"

Eve narrowed her eyes. "Me, or my dog?"

He put a hand to his chest in embarrassed surprise. "Oh, Eve, *salut*. I didn't see you—"

She held her fingers out like claws. "Are you ticklish? I *will* tickle you."

"Nooo." He leaned toward the opposite side of the phaeton. "Never tickle the driver!"

She inched closer. "I'll tickle you right out of this carriage."

He kissed the tip of her nose before she could move away.

Duenna pawed at his knee.

"All right, all right, no touching," he assured her.

Eve leaned back into the seat and closed her eyes as the cool breeze teased new tendrils free from her chignon.

Bastien could watch her all day.

She opened her eyes and smiled. "The paper is coming together. The back and inner pages are finalized. I'll arrange the front once I've finished the last article."

His article.

After so many years of accepting his status

of *not good enough* to be more than a passing fancy to the English ladies that came through the village, a strange feeling blossomed in his chest whenever Eve's interested gaze met his. She not only found him "good enough" to come back for more, she even felt his smithy was amazing enough to write about in a paper that went out to thousands of subscribers.

"Thank you for helping." The words came out steady enough. "I suppose I should also thank your father for creating the Gazette in the first place."

"No." Her eyes were on the road, her voice almost too soft to hear. "That was me, too."

How had he not realized that? "It's *your* paper?"

"No," she said again. "It's Father's paper. It was my idea. It took months to convince him. I would have done it on my own, if I'd had the means and authority. I was too young to own anything and didn't have a penny to invest."

"Can't you buy it back from him now?"

"I still don't have a penny. It's Father's paper." She continued to stare at the road. "It doesn't matter."

It did matter. He could see it mattered. It was her idea, her work, her paper.

"I'm just happy he believed in me enough

to try it." Her lips tightened. "We needed to do something. We had no income. Unpaid accounts were piling up, and my dowry was just sitting there doing nothing anyway..."

Bastien stopped the carriage. "Your father used your *dowry* to start the Gazette?"

She shrugged. "As I said, no one else was asking for it."

Eve had asked for it, Bastien would wager. The Gazette was her idea. She would have wanted to start it using her own investment.

"So," he said slowly, "your father stole your dowry and your idea—"

"I *gave* him the idea, and the dowry came from my mother. It was never mine." Her eyes blinked quickly. "If you're implying that we would have lost everything if it hadn't worked, you're right. But it did work. We've made the money back and more."

Bastien guided the horses toward the park in silence. *"We"* hadn't reaped the profit. Her father had.

"Every penny we earn goes to both of us," she said as if reading his mind. "Just as it would if *I* owned the paper."

Probably true. Bastien still wouldn't characterize the proceedings as fair to Eve, but he understood her stance of *family first*. He lived by the same tenet.

"I'm glad it worked."

"Me, too. Before we began, we could no longer afford our utterly exhausted maid-of-all-work, who barely slept four hours a night —and that was with me putting in the same hours. Now we have two maids and a foot-man, and everyone sleeps through the night."

He slanted her a look. "All you have to do is run, write, print, ship, and maintain the Cressmouth Gazette?"

"It's almost too easy." She grinned, then arched her brows knowingly. "It's not work if it's something you love to do, is it, blacksmith?"

"I wasn't born to scorch my sleeves in a forge," he protested. "I was born to spend six hours a day primping at my *toilette*."

Her lips quirked. "One more hour than Brummell?"

"*Amateur*," Bastien scoffed.

"If you could, you'd spend six hours a day in front of your looking-glass and then seven helping people in your smithy."

"Probably." He stroked his chin as though in deep thought. "Do you think I could talk Lucien into hanging the smithy walls with mirrors, in order to do both at the same time?"

"He would love it," she assured him. "All those reflections would give him even more objects to sulk at."

"Brilliant! You do have the best ideas." He steered the horses through the park.

Duenna let out a bark just as Eve pointed toward the lake.

"The swans are migrating south. They'll be gone before the paper goes to print. It looks like there are only seven left."

He lifted the reins. "Should I stop so you can interview them? Where's your notebook?"

To his surprise, she neither laughed nor smacked him on the head with said notebook. Instead she glared at the beautiful pond in an uncanny resemblance to Lucien.

"I was teasing," Bastien said quickly. "Those swans don't look newsworthy."

"They're not. That's the problem." Eve spun to face him, her green eyes flashing passionately. "Cressmouth is so much more than swans and partridges, shortbread and biscuits, holly and mistletoe. We're *people*. We all have stories. I want to be the one who helps tell them."

He frowned. "Aren't you doing so?"

"I'm trying." She let out a deep sigh. "Father thinks the Cressmouth Gazette should only talk about Christmas. When will the snow fall? How much for sleigh rides? What is on the bill at the winter theatre? Are there printed lyrics for caroling? It's the same questions every year, and he's right—they're good questions that deserve good answers. But the Gazette is a *newspaper*, not a seasonal manual. That can be a part of it, but shouldn't be everything."

"I assume you've mentioned your concerns?"

"Ad nauseum." She drummed her fingers atop the side of the phaeton. "He doesn't agree."

He sent her a pointed look. "So what are you going to do about it?"

The corner of her mouth curved up.

"Write it anyway," she admitted. "He has to approve the type before we print, so I can't turn the Gazette into a forceful wellspring of exposés and emotional, heart-warming sagas overnight, but I'm going to chip away at it bit by bit, article by article, until the Gazette truly represents all that Cressmouth is and can offer."

She was going to be phenomenal at it. Her

love for this village and her passion for telling its stories came through with every word. Bastien wished he would be there to see it happen.

"Can you inquire whether the management will ship copies to France?" he asked.

She pretended to think it over. "I know the woman in charge of the arrangements. I'll see what she can do."

There. That should make him happy. Remaining a name on her subscriber list ought to be good enough.

But it wasn't.

"Good morning, Beau," chorused a pair of young ladies beneath matching lacy parasols.

"*And Miss Shelling,*" Eve sang out under her breath in a saccharine tone.

Bastien picked up the pace and steered the phaeton out of the park.

"They're just…"

Just what? Flirting with him? Right in front of another woman whom they didn't bother to acknowledge, because they assumed Eve's interest was just as opportunistic and fleeting as theirs?

"They're just… practicing French because they think it's exotic," he finished. "'Beau' is one of the maybe ten French words they know."

Eve lifted her shoulder. "Then they know nine words more than me."

He cursed himself and gripped the reins tighter. Instead of dismissing the unwelcome interruption, he'd made her feel worse.

If Lucien were here, he'd point out that Eve's lack of French was yet another reason why she and Bastien were ill-suited.

Bastien didn't care that Eve wasn't French, but not *speaking* it posed problems. It was the language he used with his family. The language *everyone* used in the country he called home. She wouldn't belong there just like he didn't belong here.

"It's all right," he forced himself to say. "I never expect anyone to learn my language."

Usually people didn't even ask him about France. What he liked, what he missed most, what made it feel like home.

Eve tilted her head. "The baker claims you le Duc brothers are so vain about your nationality, he expects you to paint a French flag on the bonnet of your carriage."

"The baker is an imbecile." Bastien pointed skyward. "Phaetons don't have roofs."

She nodded gravely. "He'll be very disappointed to learn that."

Bastien's jaw worked. The baker wasn't the first one to make comments implying *otherness* was something to be hidden, to be embarrassed of, to apologize for. Bastien wasn't the least ashamed of himself, where he was, or where he came from. He was happy to prove it.

"Let's not disappoint him." He flashed a dangerous smile. "I'll paint the flag on the carriage myself. You can come to the smithy tomorrow morning to bear witness, so you can report to the baker that le Ducs are the Frenchest, most French-speaking, France-loving French people you've ever seen with your own eyes."

"This sounds like breaking news." Eve shot upright with excitement. "I don't want to bear witness. I want to come and help."

CHAPTER 9

Bastien and Eve swung their stools to the other side of the phaeton in the middle of the smithy. Morning sun poured in the open doors, bathing the all-black phaeton door with light.

It wouldn't be all black for long.

In exchange for reducing the outstanding amount on a blacksmithing IOU, Bastien had managed to procure several different vials of pre-mixed paint from the local colorist, who was responsible for the bright cheeriness of the village doors and exteriors.

These weren't *precisely* the right colors, but nor was Bastien *precisely* an artist. Or even sort of an artist. Luckily, the primary requirement was no more complex than the ability to draw a rectangle.

Eve leaned forward. "Which one is this?"

"This," Bastien replied, "is the *Tricolore*. It became the national flag in 1790, the year after my family fled France."

Although only distantly in line to a title, by 1789 his parents had become alarmed at the direction and frequency of the executions around them. They'd bundled up seven-year-old Lucien, four-year-old Bastien, and two-year-old Désirée, and came to England to visit Uncle Jasper until the revolution blew over.

"Did you never see it?" Eve asked.

"I did."

In 1791, there had been a brief time during which his family thought they might save their lands. They'd traveled back for that express purpose, but winter slowed them, and their arrival was too late. Désirée was too young to remember the look on their parents' faces, but Lucien and Bastien would never forget.

Soon after, their distant relation Louis-Philippe became the duc d'Orléans. But there was no time to petition for favors. Le duc d'Orléans was desperately trying to secure his brothers' release from captivity. The revolution was ongoing.

So they waited for the right moment.

They should have stayed in Cressmouth. If they had, the whole family would still be alive.

"How is the paper coming?" he asked to change the subject.

Her face lit up, as she began explaining about the finished pages whose designs she was already setting into type. Bastien tried to keep his focus on the blue stripe, the white stripe, the red stripe, but no matter how hard he tried, his gaze kept returning to Eve.

He loved how animated she became when she talked about the words she wrote, and the emotions she hoped they engendered in her readers. She was already beautiful, but her enthusiasm and obvious joy made her even more magnetic.

She let out a sigh. "Am I foolish to hope I can mold the Gazette into something meaningful?"

"Not at all." He finished the last stroke. "Sometimes hope is the most precious gift we can have."

"I just want to be taken seriously." Her eyes grew distant. "Then maybe I could stop bad things from happening."

He put down his brush and frowned. "Is something bad about to happen?"

"I don't know." She bit her lip. "Bad things always happen."

Bastien tilted his head. He'd been immersed in his own loss and the repercussions of tragedy for so long that he hadn't stopped to consider that other people suffered loss, too. People like Eve.

"Tell me what happened," he said softly.

At first, she stared down into the jar of red paint in her hands as if the answers were contained within.

"My mother." She did not lift her head. "She was ill; we knew she was ill. We should have got her a physician, a real one. We thought we did, but... All he wanted to do was bleed the fever and apply more leeches, always more leeches, but no matter how engorged they became, Mother never got better. I told Father I didn't think..."

"You didn't have faith in the physician?"

"I did at first," she admitted. "We all did. Mother and Father, too. But she kept growing weaker, and I began to have doubts. I pulled Father aside and told him I feared our savior was a sham."

"What did he say?"

Her smile was bitter and did not reach her eyes. "What would I know about such things? I was a girl. They were men. Had I attended St. Bart's medical school? My opinion meant nothing. I should leave things in the competent hands of professionals."

His stomach tightened with dread. "What happened?"

"She died." Eve's voice was flat. "And as it turned out, our doctor had no experience at all. It was a swindle."

"That is horrifying. But it's certainly not your fault." Bastien reached for her hand. "If anything, it's another fine reason for me to grab your father by the—"

"The physician was going to marry me." Her countenance was pale, her green eyes tortured. "I was sixteen and had never left Cressmouth. He was thirty and from London. He seemed impossibly wise and elegant and sophisticated. He wanted me and my dowry. So I invited him into our lives." Her voice broke. "And he took one."

Bastien hauled her to him. "That blackguard deserves to rot in gaol."

"He is." She took a shuddering breath. "Father believes in following rules and paying the consequences. He would have scorched the earth raining vengeance upon anyone who had a hand in Mother's death, if the law allowed it."

Bastien held her tighter. Now he understood. Her mother had lost her life, and Eve had lost her dowry, and everything it represented. The ability to make choices, to control her own life. The possibility of marriage, of finding love. Any hope of ever fully regaining her father's trust.

And she thought she deserved it.

He tilted her chin to face him. Her gaze was glassy and hollow.

"It is not your fault, do you hear me?" he said fiercely. "Your mother's death was *not your fault.*"

"I invited him in," she whispered. "Insisted upon deferring to his medical expertise. Father said I was too young to know my own mind, and if I would have listened..."

"*No.*" Bastien's voice was harsh because he'd lived through this self-torture himself. "You *were* young. You *didn't* know. This charlatan deceived your entire family. You cannot flay yourself alive over a past you cannot change."

Like all the tiny decisions that had ended with his parents' heads rolling away from their bodies. What if they'd stayed in Cressmouth? What if they'd gone home sooner, repossessed their land, hid in a secure location? What if they'd sided with the revolutionaries, or at least pretended to long enough to stay alive?

That way lay madness. He should know.

"Listen to me." He cupped her soft face in his hands and brought his gaze close to hers. "If there's one thing I know for certain—"

"What is the meaning of this?" thundered an angry male voice.

"Father," Eve gasped, and jerked out of Bastien's arms. "We were just—"

"I can see what you were 'just,' and you shall do no such thing." A dour white-haired man with a walking-stick and a scowl strode forward and grabbed her by the arm.

Bastien leapt to his feet. "Sir, if you'd let me explain—"

"I know everything I need to know about you and your kind." Mr. Shelling's lip curled in the direction of the phaeton as though the sight of the French flag was just as abhorrent as the thought of his daughter in a Frenchman's arms. "That's enough, Eve. The story is over."

Mr. Shelling let go of his daughter's arm

seconds before Bastien was about to stalk forward and rip his hand away.

Eve walked beside him with wooden legs, a chastised marionette hanging from her strings.

Even Duenna slunk behind with her tail between her legs.

Bastien curled his shaking hands into fists and slammed them atop the closest table. He couldn't go after her. That was her father. The only family Eve had left. Bastien couldn't—*wouldn't*—force himself between them.

Not physically.

But he had to do something to get her out of that appalling situation. *No.* That was high-handedness talking. "Bastien knew best," no better than her overbearing father.

Eve deserved *choices*.

He closed the smithy and headed straight for the castle. When the town's founder died, the old man's will and testament left Marlowe Castle and its wealth in a trust overseen by Mr. Thompson, the castle solicitor. As guardian, Mr. Thompson's power was limited, but he was far from impotent.

More importantly, Mr. Thompson believed in women. There had been until recently a female managing the counting-house.

The vacancy had been long filled and Bastien doubted Eve would have wanted it anyway, but surely there was *someone* who would recognize her worth and pay her for her work.

If she chose to remain under her father's thumb, Bastien would support her. But if she wanted to make her own way, however that might look and whatever that might mean...

He would move heaven itself to make her wish come true.

CHAPTER 10

By the following afternoon, Eve and her father had mastered the art of walking past each other with open contempt, the thump of his walking-stick and the grinding of her teeth the only sounds amongst the deafening silence of mutual disappointment.

But Eve was tired of silence. Of not being heard. Of doing absolutely everything that was within her power to do, and still not garnering enough respect or autonomy to live her own bloody life.

This time, when her father passed the drawing room without looking at her, she placed herself directly in his path.

"I'm an adult."

Her father did not bother to hide his annoyance. "You're four-and-twenty."

"Exactly." She drew herself up straight. "Yet you treat me like a child."

He leaned on his walking-stick impatiently. "You're *my* child."

"I'm your daughter, not a rag doll to be dragged about by the arm." The memory tightened her throat with shame. "You embarrassed me."

Father barked a dismissive laugh. "You embarrassed *me*. I went to buy bread, and the baker mentioned you'd been seen frolicking about the village in that Frenchman's phaeton—"

"Is that the problem? That Bastien is French?" She stepped forward, fingers tight. "Would we be having the same conversation if he was English?"

Father sniffed. "I don't care if he's from the moon. He's not good enough for you."

"How do you know he's not good enough?" Even as she asked the question, the answer punched into her chest.

Because the last man you fell for never intended to stay. The last time you swore you'd found a "good" one, someone we cared for died.

Father didn't have to say the words. They hung in the air between them.

"Bastien isn't like that." Except for the leaving part. "He's good and honest, caring and trustworthy."

"Concentrate on the Gazette. Type has to be set this week in order to print and ship before the first of November."

"I *know* how to run the Gazette. I've been setting type and meeting dates for years without your help. I also know how to run my own life."

"You clearly do not. Rules are rules, Eve, and the rule is: Stay away from Sébastien le Duc. I forbid it."

He *forbade* it? Her nostrils flared. Well, she didn't accept his proscription! Every beat of her heart rebelled against it. She was going to lose Bastien in a few weeks, but not *yet*. Not because her father dismissed him out of hand without bothering to seek the truth.

She ground her teeth. "Just because I—"

Father turned before Eve could finish her thought, dismissing her mid-sentence. He strode into his study and shut the door without a backward glance.

Her shaking fingers curled into fists. What

the devil did he even *do* in his study all day? The Gazette provided the family's only source of income, and *she* was the one who ran it. Without Eve, he wouldn't even have that luxury!

She snatched her pelisse from its wooden peg and stalked out of the front door.

Duenna joined her, tail wagging.

"We're going to see Bastien," Eve informed her, though the bullmastiff hadn't asked. If anything, she'd seemed to assume as much. Her paws pointed in the direction of the smithy without question.

The brisk walk in the cold air, surrounded by the sun setting on Cressmouth's rolling autumn beauty helped rub away some of her hurt and anger.

Father was never going to change. People never truly did. She could either resign herself to a life that was never any different than it was at this moment, or she could follow her passions and seize joy wherever she could find it.

Eve chose the latter.

When she and Duenna reached the smithy, the doors were closed. The walking path to one side led to the cottage nestled next to the woods behind the smithy. Might Bastien be at home? Well, she hadn't disobeyed her father's prohibitive edicts just to turn back now.

As they neared the cottage, a shadow moved on one side and Duenna dashed forward to investigate.

Eve picked up her hem and gave chase before her bullmastiff could tackle some innocent gardener or scullery maid out picking carrots.

She drew up short.

The shadow was not a maid or a gardener, but an enormous hog whose spine was as high as Eve's waist. The impressive girth indicated this pig weighed about three times as much as Eve and Duenna put together.

Undeterred, Duenna pranced about the pig at a safe distance, barking in delight.

A window opened.

Bastien's eyes laughed at her. "That's Chef. He won't eat Duenna, if you want to come inside."

Cheeks burning at being caught skulking outside his house when she'd actually come to apologize for her father's rude behavior, Eve left Duenna to play with the pig and made her way to the front of the cottage.

When she arrived, Bastien stood in the

open doorway, lounging against the wooden frame.

"I'm sorry about yesterday," she blurted. "Father had no right to assume—"

"Didn't he?" His brows arched sardonically. "Your father misinterpreted the situation, but he wasn't wrong about me. I *have* taken liberties with you without any promises for the future."

"So did I," she reminded him. "And I'd do it again."

"Then by all means..." He stepped back from the door. "Come inside."

Eve stepped into a beautiful entryway. Although the exterior of the le Ducs' cozy home looked no different from the other cottages, the interior managed to look rich and elegant without the presence of ostentatious gewgaws or blatant displays of wealth.

Bastien caught her gaze. "Not my handiwork, I'm afraid. Désirée and Carole are the ones responsible for the men not living like the pig."

Carole was Carole Quincy, the friend who not only created the swan woodcut for the Gazette, but had also designed the Duke of Azureford's billiards room. She would make an excellent subject to interview for the spring issue. Eve pulled out her journal to jot a note.

Bastien stared at her. "If you're adding 'would sleep with the pig' to my article…"

She burst out laughing. "No one would believe it if I did. You're the closest Cressmouth has to an out-and-out dandy."

"*Close* to a dandy?" His spine straightened in faux offense as he looped a worn kitchen apron about his neck. "You find me merely *close* to sartorial perfection?"

She thought him close to perfection full stop, but restrained her reply to a cheeky grin as she followed him into the kitchen.

He glanced over his shoulder. "Are you hungry?"

The delicious scents of thyme and garlic hit her nose.

Her stomach growled in response.

He pointed to a wooden stool. "Sit. I'm going to feed you."

She sent him a startled look, heart pounding. "You are?"

"Duenna is in the garden with Chef." He lowered his voice to a whisper. "You do *not* want him in charge of your supper."

She sat, and rested her elbows on the table to watch him.

"*Coq au vin*," he explained. "Almost ready. It takes just over two hours."

"Have you considered you were destined to be a cook rather than a blacksmith?"

He rolled his eyes. "And perform on cue as some English aristocrat's prized French chef?"

"You dislike aristocrats?"

"How can I, when…" He busied himself serving the fragrant braised chicken.

Her chest kicked with sudden understanding. "You're an aristocrat?"

"No," he said quickly. When she didn't look away, he sighed and met her gaze. "With luck, I'll never be. Lucien is the first in line."

Eve's mouth fell open. No wonder he was eager to return to France.

All this time, her father was right. She and Bastien *were* poorly matched. But not because he wasn't good enough for her. *She* was the one whose status was beneath *his*.

"It's the worst thing that could have happened to us," he warned her. "That's why my parents were killed in Southern Brittany during the so-called 'peasant revolt.' They were unapologetic royalists."

Royalists believed in dividing people into classes, passing the power from father to firstborn son. Of course they would not back a rebellion that sought to redistribute their advantages to ordinary, lower class citizens.

She itched to pull out her notebook and ask a thousand questions. Forget the smithy. *This* was a story that would get people talking. Conflict and controversy, politics and emotion. When did unequal privilege become *too much* power? Was violence ever the right answer?

"That must have been terrifying," she said softly.

His gaze was raw. "I was ten that day. Old enough to understand what had happened, but not old enough to understand why. Désirée was even younger. At thirteen, Lucien suddenly became the head of our family."

She covered his hand with hers and squeezed.

His smile did not reach his eyes. "The servants left. We had no access to funds. Perhaps they wouldn't have stayed even if we could pay them. Our pantry was well-stocked, not that we had any idea what to do with any of it. The night Uncle Jasper came, Lucien had sliced open his finger trying to filet a fish, and Désirée was sitting in the middle of her room crying because she couldn't untangle her hair."

Eve's voice softened. "Where were you?"

"Sewing Lucien's finger." Bastien fingered the hem of his jacket. "I got better at sewing. All three of us learned to cook. But back then, we were scared, grieving children who had been on our own for all of four days, and were failing horribly."

"But your uncle came." She could not imagine what walking into such a scene must have felt like. Or how earth-shattering it must have been to have everything one moment and nothing the next.

Bastien inclined his head. "Uncle Jasper gathered us up and everything of value we could carry, and we left that very night. He brought us back here, because there was nowhere else for us to go."

Thank God for Cressmouth. It was just the miracle they needed.

Sort of.

"That's when Mr. Marlowe forced your family to sign a predatory lease?" she remembered.

He shook his head. "Uncle Jasper signed willingly. It was that, or sleep on the floor in the smithy."

"Just because you choose to do something

doesn't mean you truly had another choice," she said quietly.

Bastien picked up their empty plates and carried them to the basin without comment.

She followed. "What happens when you go back?"

"We don't know. Now that the Bourbon monarchy is restored, Lucien is petitioning for the return of our land. Others have had some success, and he is hopeful we will, too."

She frowned at this phrasing. "You're not hopeful, too?"

He shrugged. "I don't need land. I was born to be a dandy with no other cares or skills, and instead I became a dandy who can forge iron, harvest vegetables, feed pigs, season chicken, and sew a bloody fine seam. We *want* our birthright, but we don't *need* it. We can survive anywhere."

And the place he'd chosen was France.

She pretended the reminder didn't claw a hole in her chest. "When are you leaving?"

"The morning of Epiphany. I've sent away for passage."

Of course he had. He'd been waiting for this opportunity for years. *Freedom,* to live where he wished, to do as he pleased. Who wouldn't be counting down the days?

Maybe she should do so, too. They had a finite number of hours in which to enjoy each other's company.

She let her gaze linger on the muscles of his upper arm, on the breadth of his strong shoulders, on the thrilling familiarity of his wide, firm mouth and how sensual it had felt against her own.

He caught her staring. His eyes lowered to her parted lips. She licked them. His gaze heated.

Neither of them were thinking about Christmas or pigs or a sea passage anymore. The only thought in her mind was that an arm's length away from her was much too far for him to be. She wanted his kisses. Yearned for his embrace. If he was waiting for a sign… she'd give him one.

"Dessert?" he managed, his voice a raspy growl.

Absolutely. She lifted on her toes and pressed her lips to his.

This kiss was different than the ones before. They *knew* each other now. Not just in the sense of two people whose mouths had entwined in passion on multiple occasions, but as two people who were no longer afraid to show their true selves.

He knew how much she loved the Gazette yet felt stifled by it; how much she loved her father yet felt stifled by *him*. Bastien didn't pat her on the head for having aspirations or suggest the only thing missing in her life was a husband to take over all the pesky thinking. He trusted her to think for herself. He thought her talented, capable. Attractive.

Heaven knew no man could hold a candle to Sébastien le Duc. He wasn't afraid to bare himself fully. Iron calluses, scullery work, a jacket molded so perfectly to his muscled frame that any pink of the ton would weep to have such tailoring in their own wardrobe.

He seemed to believe she would think these things betrayed his inferiority, but they only made him more real. More special.

She ran her hands up those hard muscles and locked her arms about him tight.

"Eve," he said between drugging kisses. "I'd kiss you for the next straight fortnight if I could."

Her heart skipped. "But?"

"But..." He kissed both corners of her mouth. "We're standing in my kitchen and I don't live alone."

Oh, God. Her pulse jumped. His family

could walk in at any moment. "Is there somewhere else we can go?"

He held her gaze, his brown eyes dark with passion, then his mouth crushed hers. They were no longer standing in the kitchen, but bouncing against a wall, weaving down a narrow corridor, lurching through an open doorway.

Bastien kicked the door closed, engaged the lock, and then his arms were wrapped around her once more. She melted against him. He was so *there*, so solid, the rest of the world seemed like a faded watercolor in comparison. His kisses stole her breath and her heart, leaving her no choice but to surrender.

They tumbled backward toward a soft mattress, but she was already falling, had already fallen. Her equilibrium had vanished the first time he'd kissed her. She was here because there was nowhere else she'd rather be; no one she'd rather be with; nothing else she'd rather be doing than drowning in his kisses.

Eve showed him with her hands and mouth and tongue the words she dare not admit aloud.

She *loved* him.

There was no other explanation for giddiness at the sight of him, the yearning when they were apart, the terror at the thought of losing him forever. He'd lived down the road for the past eighteen years, and somehow she had just found him. Every moment before their first kiss was wasted time. She would not waste the time they had left.

She had always promised herself that if she ever met a man who respected her enough to trust her with complete honesty, a man she could trust with anything at all... she'd hold back nothing.

When his fingers skated so, so close to the nipples straining against her bosom, she grasped his hair and demanded, "*Touch me.*"

Again, the fingers circling, teasing, but not quite reaching. "Where?"

"Everywhere."

Rather than cup her through the linen, he tugged the hem of her bodice below her breast and captured the sensitive peak with his mouth.

She gasped in pleasure. This was not what she expected. This was not even something she'd known she *could* expect. This was so much better.

Without lifting his mouth from her bosom, he yanked up her skirts just far enough to slide his hand beneath and—*ohhh*, yes. Exactly there.

Had she thought his mouth and tongue delicious torture? What his fingers were now doing had her panting, writhing, bucking, pleading for a release she'd only ever found home alone in her bedchamber. It was about to happen *here*. With him.

Margaret loved to tease that Eve didn't know what she was missing. Now was just the perfect time to find out. Bastien was the only man Eve wanted to find out *with*.

Even if she could only have him for a short while, every stolen moment together was well worth the future heartache. Tonight, she would finally find out what she'd be missing when he left…

And so would he.

CHAPTER 11

Bastien's breeches were so tight he feared his fall might burst open on its own, flinging buttons left and right as his arousal broke free from its restraints. Or perhaps it was Bastien who was ripping away the feeble wisps of propriety that had kept them from stealing anything more than a kiss.

Eve didn't want restrained kisses. Her fingers twisted in his hair, locking him to her breast, as though there was anywhere else he'd rather be.

Perhaps there was.

Her erotic little moans and the irresistible way she writhed against his stroking fingers indicated she was very close to the precipice. He wanted to be there to taste it.

He left his hand where it was and lowered his mouth between her legs.

"Sébastien," was all she managed before coming apart.

Only when the last tremor faded did he kiss his way up her body, over her chest, up the curve of her neck, then lay down beside her.

She frowned. "What are you doing?"

"Cuddling you." He stopped. "You don't like it?"

"I adore it. But can we do it… afterward?"

"After…" His throat dried.

She wasn't done with him. She was just getting started.

He touched her cheek. "Eve…"

She untied his cravat. Rather than toss the linen square aside, she left it hanging about his neck and used both corners to pull him to her.

An excellent rebuttal. Now that his body pressed against hers and their mouths were locked in a kiss, Bastien was completely incapable of heroically summoning a single whisper of restraint.

By all accounts, Eve should not give herself to him but hold out for marriage—or at least someone who would still be here in the new year. He was not the man her father hoped she'd find, and they both knew it.

But she was also *Eve*. Who should be in charge of her life, but her? Should her limitations be what others placed upon her, or what she herself wished to have and to do? She wanted him. He wanted her. This moment was about pleasing each other, not the rest of the world.

And there was nothing he wanted more than to please her.

If his kisses were hungrier than before, his movements more urgent, it was because now that he realized they *could* have it all, he didn't want to waste a single moment.

Why was she still wearing a dress? *Gone.* That flimsy linen shift? Gone. His waistcoat, shirt, breeches? Gone, gone, gone. Now there was nothing between them, not even a breath of cool air. Just heated flesh against heated flesh, rubbing, touching, teasing, kissing, tasting.

When he nudged within her at last, fingers entwined atop the pillow, her hands tightened on his and a slight gasp interrupted their kiss.

He paused, his heart twisting. He hadn't meant to hurt her; had never been in a situation where it might happen. But already her kisses were impatient, her thighs relaxed and welcoming.

She wrapped her legs about his hips and all control was lost. His only goal was to coax her to the peak again, to send her flying over, and then to join her in succumbing completely to pleasure.

Only after she breathed his name a second time and clamped her muscles around him in ecstasy, did he allow himself several uninhibited thrusts of absolute heaven before burying his hips in the blanket beside her and muffling his moan in the pillow.

Spent, he flung an arm over her, curled himself about her softness, and pressed a kiss to the top of her head. He closed his eyes, breathing in her scent and enjoying her warmth as he drifted half in and out of consciousness.

He would have happily held her snuggled close to his chest all night long, had her dog not chosen that moment to release an ear-piercing howl just outside Bastien's bedchamber window.

"*Duenna.*" Eve sprang out of his arms in a heartbeat. "I have to go."

She was tucked away inside her shift and

her gown faster than Bastien could pull on his shirt and breeches.

Was she happy? Horrified? Embarrassed?

He hopped after her with one boot on and the other clutched in his hand. "Eve—"

But she was out the door and gone, her dog bounding along beside her.

Bastien leaned against the wall to tug on his other boot, but did not give chase after her. If she wanted to go, that was her choice. If she'd wanted him to come with her, she would have said. If she regretted their intimacy, he would not press unwelcome advances upon her. If she'd enjoyed every moment and wished to do it again…

Well, his calendar could be made free tomorrow.

Lucien walked around the corner and glared at him. "Why is the door open?"

"I was… looking outside."

"We have windows." Lucien arched a brow. "And it is dark."

Bastien reached for the door handle, then paused to see two figures striding down the path toward the cottage, one in skirts and the other in a tailcoat. His hands went clammy.

Lucien narrowed his eyes. "*Qu'est-ce que c'est?*"

"I might have just..." Bastien lifted a shaking hand to tug nervously upon his cravat, only to realize it still lay discarded on his bedchamber floor. "Er..."

"Is it too late at night for a neighborly visit?" called out a cheerful female voice.

Was it possible to have an apoplexy out of *relief?* Bastien's heart was certainly making the attempt. The unexpected visitors were not Eve and her father after all, but Olive Harper and her father Gilbert from the stud farm next door.

Lucien crossed his arms rather than respond. He understood the question, but hated to appear less than perfect in anything. Lucien would rather be judged sulky or a misanthrope than to falter in his English. He believed displaying one's vulnerabilities to be a sign of weakness, and did not realize that by *practicing* his English with the people he was so careful to avoid, he might rid himself of the supposed weakness altogether.

"Come in, come in." Bastien welcomed them grandly. "We haven't any tea, but we do have several chairs and a warm fire."

"We didn't come for tea," Olive said once they were settled in the parlor. "We'd like to make an offer."

Lucien leaned forward. *"Une bonne offre?"*

"What kind of offer?" Bastien relaxed into his chair.

"For the smithy." She folded her hands in her lap and named a number.

The stiff sides of Bastien's wingback chair were the only thing that had prevented him from tumbling to the floor. He had worked out a best-case price and a worst-case price, and Olive's number was barely a percentage shy of the best-case price.

"Oui," Lucien hissed. "Tell her *yes.*"

He was right. This would be more than enough money to purchase a small *gîte* in France to live in while they awaited the outcome of their petition.

Bastien crossed his arms. No one in the Harper family was a blacksmith. "What would you do with the smithy?"

Lucien stared at him as though he'd lost his mind. "Who cares? We will be *in France.*"

Bastien cared. If they sold the smithy to someone who couldn't keep it open... what would happen to Cressmouth?

Olive made several hurried gestures to her father.

He responded in kind.

Although Bastien didn't comprehend the

rapid hand signs, he never minded watching them converse silently. If anything, Olive's relationship with her father held similarities to Bastien's relationship with Lucien. Neither Lucien nor Mr. Harper could speak for themselves, but they very much still deserved to be an equal part of the conversation.

Olive turned back to Bastien. "We'll find a blacksmith to rent it from us at a profit."

They intended to make a similar bargain to the one Mr. Marlowe had made with Uncle Jasper. Only with the Harpers, Bastien suspected they would include a possibility for the new lessee to gain financial independence.

"*Magnifique.*" Lucien stared daggers at Bastien. "Sell it."

"I need a fortnight," Bastien answered in English.

Olive arched her brows. "Has there been another offer?"

"Not yet," he admitted. "But we've an advertisement placed in the next Gazette, which ships on Tuesday. If there's no interest within a fortnight, we'll take your offer."

"And if there is interest?"

"All things being equal, we prefer to sell to a blacksmith."

"I do not prefer!" Lucien hissed. "We prefer *money*."

Olive made more gestures to her father.

He gestured back and gave a smug smile.

This time when Olive turned around, the number she named matched Bastien's best-case calculations to the penny.

"*Yes*," Lucien croaked in heavily accented but perfectly understandable English.

"*No*," Bastien said just as firmly.

He hated gainsaying his brother, particularly at such a vital moment when Lucien had finally risked speaking his first word of English in front of actual English people, but Bastien could not chance that the best case for *les frères* le Duc resulted in the worst case for Cressmouth.

He was willing to leave this village behind, not leave it in shambles.

"A fortnight," he said in a tone that brooked no argument. "I will give you the courtesy of making a counteroffer before we sign any contracts."

Olive pushed to her feet and her father did the same. They did not appear to be perturbed in any way.

As next-door neighbors, the Harpers and le Ducs had always shared a friendly, easy relationship. And as the richest full-time residents, the Harpers didn't *need* the smithy. They could make virtually any investment they wished anywhere in England. They were intelligent enough not to make an offer unless it was a wise business decision for the family, but they were also considerate enough to direct their wealth in an act of kindness toward their neighbors.

As soon as they were gone, Lucien spun toward Bastien. "What is wrong with you?"

"A fortnight is just fourteen days," Bastien reminded him. "We'll be here for six more weeks. We have the time to do this correctly. Now that our new 'worst case' has become 'accept every penny we'd ever hoped for from the Harpers,' isn't it worth a mere fortnight to see if we can get an even better 'best case?'"

Instead of glaring in response, the corners of Lucien's eyes crinkled, and he grinned at his brother.

"You did it!" He clapped Bastien on the shoulder and all but danced about the entryway. "If it's the worst case, we leave the morning after Twelfth Night as planned with the Harpers' gold in our pockets. If it's best case, we won't even *need* it. Louis-Philippe will help restore our land, and we can spend the rest of our lives doing anything we want."

Anything he wanted. Bastien certainly liked the sound of that. Except, anytime he tried to picture exactly what he wanted…

All he could see was Eve.

CHAPTER 12

When Eve returned home from the market the following afternoon, her father was waiting for her at the front door with his walking-stick in one hand and her test print of the Gazette's front page in the other.

His face was purple.

He shook the wrinkled test print at her as she hefted her purchases onto the closest table.

"What is the meaning of this?" he demanded.

"That," she answered calmly, "is the front page of the December Cressmouth Gazette."

"Not anymore." He crumpled the paper into a ball and hurled it into the fire. "I removed that ridiculous article from the type."

"You *what?*" Eve whirled to face him, no longer calm in the slightest. "I spent *all night* setting and perfecting that type!"

"You said you were going to write about *locals*." Father's eyes flashed. "Not the le Duc brothers."

She pointed out the window. "Their smithy is half a mile down the road. They're *local*."

His jaw was set. "They're not from here."

"They are now!" Her muscles tightened at the unfairness.

"Not for long," Father pointed out with satisfaction. "You said it yourself in your little article. Their home is France, not England, and they're finally going back to where they belong."

Her hands shook. "That is *not* what I said."

Now more than ever she wanted her story to run on the front page, just to prove her father wrong.

Eve lifted her chin. "Bastien and Lucien are good people, and they're important members of this community."

"The Cressmouth Gazette is supposed to please everyone." He spoke as though she was a child. "They read it to hear about *Christmas*. No one cares about the le Duc family."

She stared at him. "You cannot make base-less assumptions about people just because they happen to be French. *You* might not show interest in their family, but plenty of others do. The Le Ducs *matter*. Literally half our village crowded into the castle chapel for a glimpse of Désirée le Duc's wedding."

"Then write about weddings, if our sub-scribers must have idle gossip with their holiday cheer. And if the subject need be a duke... Why not Azureford?"

Her jaw tightened. "His Grace's wedding was a month ago."

Father continued undeterred. "How about... the Duke of Nottingvale?"

"He's not even here," Eve bit out. "His annual Christmastide house party isn't until *Christmas*."

"But he could fall in love at his party once he does arrive." Father wriggled his brows. "Speculate on that. He's an Englishman and an aristocrat. It'll be a lovely article."

"Publicly speculate on the fictional marital interests of the very real, very powerful Duke of Nottingvale?" She let out a dry laugh. "That's not an article, Father. That's a lawsuit. He'll shut the Cressmouth Gazette down if I invent 'false news' about him."

"It won't matter." Father shrugged without meeting her gaze. "This is our last issue anyway."

"*What?*" She staggered backward, her pulse skittering in horror.

It couldn't be the last issue! The Cressmouth Gazette was Eve's *life*.

"I'm old." He lifted his walking-stick. "I'm in pain."

"But I do everything!" Her voice sounded tinny and desperate, even to her own ears. "I write, I design, I set the type… The inking and printing takes two people, and Margaret often helps. But now that we have a footman, I can ask Anderson—"

"We have better odds of being able to keep our footman by ending the Gazette," Father said wearily. "I am five-and-sixty. I'm more than ready to retire from responsibilities, but our household needs money. The paper turns a small profit, but we spend so much on shipping and materials that we would actually be wealthier if we sold the printing press and have done."

"I don't want to 'have done,'" she stammered. "You can retire, and I'll run it by myself. I'll be our footman too, if I have to be. Just let me—"

"I *am* letting you." His voice was surprisingly tender. "How many times have you told me the Gazette was your steppingstone to greener pastures? This is your chance to go find them."

Her *one* chance. The front page of the Gazette needed to be worth every single lovingly placed piece of type if she wanted a prayer of convincing a legitimate newspaper that she was capable of actual journalism.

"You're right." She struggled for breath. "'The Smithy at the Heart of Christmas' is the wrong story to run."

Father patted her on the shoulder. "I knew you'd see it my way."

What she saw was that she needed something bigger. *Much* bigger. The smithy could be part of it, but she needed a hook, a controversy, a reason for everyone to ask each other, *Have you read the article in the Cressmouth Gazette?*

She needed the le Ducs.

Heart pounding, she pushed the basket of vegetables aside. "I'm taking Duenna for a walk."

Father nodded absently. "I'll be in my study."

"What do you *do* in there?" she asked his retreating back.

He paused to toss a rueful look over his shoulder.

"Sleep," he admitted. "Lying flat isn't comfortable for me anymore, and when my joints lock, it's hard to get out of bed. But I've found if I prop myself just so in a chair with a footstool before the fire… Sometimes I can sleep for thirty or forty minutes at a time."

She stared after him wordlessly as he thumped into his study and shut the door.

He meant it, she realized. He was old, he was tired, he was in pain, and he might even think he was doing her a favor. Cutting the apron strings. Finally granting the baby bird the autonomy to fly free of the nest.

But she couldn't *do* any of those things without having proper credits to her name. Something thought-provoking and unforgettable.

Someone like Bastien.

"Come on, Duenna." She opened the front door and her bullmastiff shot out like a cannonball.

She'd write about the smithy, and why it was an important feature of the community. And with Bastien's permission, she'd also write about what brought them here in the first place. How they'd gone from heirs to blacksmiths. How commoners had murdered aristocrats like the le Ducs' parents. And, of course, she'd also explain exactly what it was the revolutionaries were fighting for.

Was England one "peasant revolt" away from equality for all? Or, like France, would royalists win out in the end? Regardless of which side one believed to be right, was violence ever the answer?

That was an article. Sensational, yet full of substance. Political and divisive. Written with both sensitivity and empathy. Editors of the broadsheets didn't have to agree with Eve's *words*. They just had to agree she could *write*. The Le Ducs weren't mere news fodder. They were people, and deserved to be treated as such.

Eve walked faster. She'd print the copies without waiting for her father's approval. Eve was the one who handled the shipping; she could start a few days early. The paper would be inked and out of the door before Father knew what she'd done.

"Good afternoon, Miss Shelling!"

Jack Skeffington's twins were trundling iron hoops in front of their house.

Eve lifted a hand to wave reflexively, then paused when Duenna barked.

Duenna never barked at the Skeffingtons. They'd lived here just as long as Eve had.

A cheroot-smoking, wind-chapped, unshaven man hefting a distinctive wooden box trudged up the front step and disappeared into the house.

"Who was that?" Eve asked with curiosity.

"Redmire," Frederick replied instantly. "He's a—"

Annie smacked her brother in the stomach, causing him to double over with a soft *oof*.

"—a businessman," she finished, smiling up at Eve angelically. "Redmire is Papa's investment associate, visiting from abroad."

There was definitely more to *that* story, but Eve didn't have time to pursue it. She had a gazette to print tomorrow morning, which meant she needed a new front page *tonight*. She'd come back to the Skeffingtons later.

"That's nice, dears. Have a good afternoon."

Eve tried to hurry Duenna down the street toward the le Duc property, but a passing squirrel sent Duenna shooting off in the opposite direction toward the park.

"*Blast.*" Eve picked up her skirts and chased after her dog.

Only when the squirrel had taken refuge high overhead, were Eve and her bullmastiff finally on their way toward the le Ducs. No, not the le Ducs…

Toward *Bastien*. A smile teased her lips.

He hadn't left her mind for a moment after the wondrous evening they'd shared in each other's arms. Tonight she would be too busy setting the paper, and tomorrow printing it, but the day after that… Her cheeks flushed with anticipation.

Once the Gazette had shipped, Eve could think of several ways she and Bastien could warm up the winter nights.

This time when she passed the Skeffington house, the children were no longer outside. In fact, the winding dirt road was empty. Eve supposed it was teatime. Perhaps she ought to have brought a basket to share with the le Ducs.

Neither Bastien nor Lucien was in the smithy, so she headed on back to their cottage and knocked upon the door.

No one answered.

Her fingernails bit into her palms. She

hadn't considered the possibility of not *finding* them in time to write her story.

"Roowwff!" Duenna scampered around the corner of the cottage and out of sight.

"Not the pig again," Eve groaned, and took off after her.

When she rounded the corner, Duenna was nowhere to be seen… but voices floated out from one of the rooms. Eve paused. The window Bastien had spoken to her through yesterday was still cracked open. She wasn't going to *eavesdrop*, but she could try to determine his voice. If he was home, she'd knock on the front door again.

A blur of lilting French sounded from behind the window.

That was… Lucien? Maybe?

A matching rumble of melodic French came in response, followed by what sounded like the snick of two ivory billiards cues hitting each other.

That one had been… Bastien? Perhaps? Speaking in French changed more than the words. Their tone became deeper, more liquid, like honey dripping from a spoon or chocolate melting in a pot.

The important thing was not how seductive Bastien sounded when he spoke French, she reminded herself. The important thing was that he was *here*, and she should go knock so they could talk about her article.

Eve stepped away from the window and moved toward the front door, only to freeze at the sight of Jack Skeffington lumbering down the path from the smithy to the cottage with a heavy box in his arms.

She gasped and flattened herself against the house where he couldn't see her. She hadn't been eavesdropping—wouldn't have been able to understand a single word even if she tried—but "skulking under the neighbor's window" was not attractive, regardless of her excuses.

His knock on the front door was much louder than hers. Nor did he wait for a butler to heed his call. He simply barged on in and kicked the door shut behind him.

"Well, if I'd known *that* was all I needed to do," Eve muttered.

But she didn't move from her hiding spot. She couldn't. Not yet. If Jack was merely dropping off that box and turning around, he'd catch her coming around the corner. And of course, there was still Duenna to deal with. No, the best course of action was—

The box. What was in the box? It was the

same size and shape and had the same distinctive markings as the box Redmire-the-business-associate had lugged in from his carriage. It had to be the same box. But of what?

New cue balls, perhaps? Everyone knew Jack played billiards with the le Ducs every week or two. People liked to tease him that he was the only Englishman Lucien le Duc could stand.

Father had not been teasing when he said things like that. That would change when the article came out, she promised herself. Father would see the le Ducs as more than just foreigners and blacksmiths, but well-rounded people with pasts and futures, tragedies and dreams. As *neighbors*.

A door squeaked, followed by a blur of French. Lucien?

"That's right, you ill-tempered goat," came Jack's voice. "We're back in business."

Eve grinned to herself as she imagined Lucien's expression.

"Redmire is a genius," came Bastien's voice. "Is that champagne, or just brandy?"

Eve frowned. Both substances were illegal, but that hadn't stopped most aristocrats from indulging anyway. Perhaps the box that Redmire delivered had been Jack's parting gift for the le Duc family. Something French, to show his support.

Lucien let loose with another stream of French.

"Obviously we'll drink it no matter what," Bastien replied, with a tone that heavily implied he was rolling his eyes at his brother. "You can't fault a man for wanting to know if we're a *little* wealthier or a *lot* wealthier."

Eve's skin went cold. Why would they… Surely he couldn't mean…

A cork popped, followed by the sound of Jack's voice. "A *lot* wealthier."

Glasses clinked.

Eve's shoulders sagged against the house.

"I hated not being able to pay you last month," Jack continued. "But I promised I'd resolve the situation, and I did. We'll ship twice as much this month, which means—"

Which meant he and the le Ducs were smugglers.

They weren't innocent, good-hearted, down-on-their-luck blacksmiths. They were *pretending* to be whilst secretly circumventing two different countries' laws for their own profit. Smuggling was considered treason against the Crown.

Her heart clanged. Her palms were cold

and sweaty. Hadn't Father warned her enough about men who hid their true selves? This wasn't some minor omission of the truth. This was a lie on the scale of *prison-for-the-rest-of-his-life*. Right there in Newgate with her previous beau.

Who knew what else he was capable of? Certainly not *trusting* her. Her eyes stung. Well, she'd just learned she couldn't trust him, either.

And she'd spent half the night naked in his embrace.

A series of tubes rattled overhead, startling her. Almost instantly, the pig began to snort… and Duenna began to bark.

CHAPTER 13

"What's wrong?" Lucien demanded, setting down his glass to stalk closer.

Bastien let out a breath. No matter how wide one smiled or how much champagne one drank, his older brother could always see through to the real Bastien.

"I'm happy about the money," he answered in French. He dug into his waistcoat pocket. "You'll be happy about these, too."

Lucien's eyes widened at the sight of the tickets.

"Ocean passage?" He clutched them to his chest as though the scraps of paper were a bouquet of roses.

Bastien should have felt the same way.

Would have felt the same way. But looking at them made him feel far more gut-punched than giddy. As it turned out, somewhere between sending for tickets home and receiving them in the post…

He'd fallen in love.

"Stop." Lucien narrowed his eyes. "Why are you not prancing around the room with me?"

Bastien placed his hands on his hips. "Dandies don't prance."

"You prance more than the Harpers' prize pony." Lucien set the tickets on the billiards table, thought better of it, and tucked them carefully into an inner pocket. "Why did you put on the spangled waistcoat if you are not going to prance?"

Because the spangled waistcoat was Bastien's favorite waistcoat. It was the nicest thing he owned, next to his new jacket—which he was also wearing. This outfit wasn't for him, but for Eve.

She hadn't asked for any promises. Hadn't delivered any ultimatums. Hadn't demanded he choose between her and his home country.

He was choosing anyway. And he chose her.

Bastien drew a deep breath and stood up straight. "I'm going to—"

"What's that?" Jack set down his champagne and put his hand to his ear.

"Feeding tubes," Lucien answered in French. "Uncle Jasper must be sending Chef his supper."

"Not *that*," Jack replied in English. He frowned. "It sounds like a dog. Do you have a dog?"

They did not have a dog. *Eve* had a dog.

Was she *here?*

Bastien abandoned his champagne and tore out of the billiards room without a word of explanation. Jack and Lucien shouldn't be the first people to hear about the feelings threatening to burst from Bastien's heart. The first person should be Eve.

He caught up with her just as she was dragging Duenna away from Chef's pen.

"I'm glad you're here," he blurted out. "I wanted to tell you—"

"—that you're a smuggler?" Her eyes flashed with anger and betrayal.

"W-what?" he stammered, his pulse skipping.

"Sorry, I don't know the French word for that. Here are some more English words: gaol, criminal, illegal, treasonous." Her eyes flashed. "Oh, here's another one: *liar*."

He drew up short. "I never lied to you."

Her laugh was short and humorless. "If you dare say to me, 'I would have told you I'm a criminal who smuggles illegal contraband in order to line my own pockets despite any risk to my neck, if only you had *asked*.' I swear I shall kill you."

He folded his arms over his chest. "You're right. I didn't tell you and I wasn't going to. How I support my family is none of your business."

Except, he'd been about to *make* it her business, hadn't he? If he'd proposed marriage to her and *then* she found out...

"It's my business now." He hadn't trusted her, and now she couldn't trust him. No, worse... she couldn't trust *herself*. All the old guilt about her role in the events leading to her mother's death came roaring back. She had sworn never to fall for a duplicitous scoundrel ever again. Her voice shook. "I came here planning to write a front page story about you, and I suppose I found a bigger one than I expected."

"*What?*" he spluttered. "You can't publish *treason!*"

"Oh, do you make *all* the rules now?" She drew herself up straighter. "The last time *I* checked, you don't control me."

Bastien's temples throbbed. He'd thought his worst fear was that she, too, would deem him not good enough. This was a hundred times worse. If she breathed a word of this before he and Lucien boarded that boat, there would be no smithy and no France. Just gaol. And possibly a noose.

"Eve." He reached for her. "Stop and think for a second."

"Like you stopped and thought?" She skipped out of reach, eyebrows shooting skyward. "Smuggling is illegal and helps fund lawlessness. Whose side are *you* on?"

Her belittling words ripped a fresh hole in his chest. Did she think he didn't *know* that illegal activity funded people who did illegal things? She had never been in a position where she had no choice but to make a hard decision at great personal risk.

Bastien would do anything for those he loved. *Anything.* He would personally sneak through caves and smuggle each bottle of brandy by hand if that's what it would have taken to keep a roof over their heads, food in his sister's belly, clothes on their backs. Of course he knew he was risking his life. His uncle had done the same for him. Those were risks he was willing to take for his family.

He wasn't going to let her throw it all away just to have her name in some quarterly Christmas gazette.

"You will ruin more than my life if you print this," he growled. "You'll ruin my brother's life. My sister's life. Jack's life. His children."

She met his gaze. Her eyes were tortured. "Journalists don't pick the news."

"I wasn't clear." He gave a brittle smile. "If you even attempt to hurt my family, I will destroy you."

Family. He had wanted that word to include Eve.

He had been foolish.

The world had already shown him what he could and could not do and be and have.

Others did not think his family deserved the privileges they had, so they tried to run. Others did not think his parents deserved their lives or their heads, so they took them. And now Eve did not think the family he had left deserved what little they had either, and intended to snatch their happiness and their future away with a stroke of her pen.

This was Bastien's fault. His family was in danger because he'd fallen in love with an Englishwoman. He slammed his fist against the doorframe.

Once again, they'd have to run.

CHAPTER 14

*E*ve did not spend the night setting type for the printing press as she'd planned. She spent the long, endless hours slumped against the empty wooden table with her head in her hands.

It was time to print the Gazette. The first batch needed to be distributed the day after tomorrow. And her front page still had a gaping hole where the smithy article had once lived.

She should be happy. Over the moon. She had what she wanted, didn't she? A story that people would notice. A way for *her* to finally be noticed. Actual journalism, credited to her name. Wasn't that the dream? Wasn't publishing articles like this exactly what she'd always thought she wanted to do for the rest of her life?

Along the way, she'd managed to fall in love with a criminal and a liar, but if she was *disappointed*, that was her own stupid fault.

From the time she was young, Father had warned her that men always had something to hide. She'd ignored him and welcomed a lying blackguard into their home, forfeiting her mother's life. Had that not been proof enough?

Barricading herself from romance by throwing herself into her love of journalism only underscored the matter. She read every single newspaper she could get her hands on, and every day of the week was more of the same: people everywhere put their wants above others' needs to disastrous effect. Men might be the bulk of the villains, but crime did not belong to them alone.

It had been foolish of her to believe Bastien to be any different. Willfully naive. He was Cressmouth's most dashing rake, and she hadn't even bothered to ask if he spent his time away from her off in the arms of someone else. How was that for first-rate investigative skills?

She hadn't *wanted* to know if there was

something to hide. She was a turtle in her shell; an ostrich with her head in the sand. Part of her had always assumed he wasn't perfect. As long as she never found out just how much, she could enjoy him while she had him, and then pick up the pieces of her heart after he was gone, none the wiser.

Except now she was wiser. And it was torture.

The door to the printing house creaked open and Duenna scampered inside, followed by Eve's father.

She didn't lift her head from her hands.

He placed a small plate of toast and cheese on the table before her and leaned on his walking-stick. "You didn't come home last night."

"I was here," she mumbled, gesturing vaguely in the direction of the press.

He walked over to the type for the front page. "Where's your article?"

"You dumped the letters back into the bucket." Was her tone bitter? Why, yes it was.

If only she could go back to how it was when *Le Duc Brothers are the Heart of Christmas* was the most pressing thing on her mind.

"I meant your new article." Father pulled out a wooden stool and sat heavily across from her. "I told you to find something else to write about."

At this, she looked up.

"I did find something else," she said, her tone polite enough to shatter glass. "Did you know Jack Skeffington has a taste for champagne and French brandy?"

Father blinked. "I... cannot claim to be shocked by this. His wine cellar is almost as legendary as the—"

"Did you know he and the le Ducs *smuggle* champagne and French brandy in some sort of long-term, intricate operation that stretches over who knows how much of England?"

Father's outraged expression indicated that no, he did not.

"That's against the law," he spluttered. "Society is built on rules. The government has made it extremely clear that—"

Eve did not listen to his tirade. She'd been subjected to variations on this theme for most of her life, and had already spent a sleepless night giving herself much the same talk.

There *were* rules. She did not want her country to descend into lawlessness. Bad enough that English soldiers were dying left and right abroad. She had no wish to encourage reckless criminal behavior here at home.

Nor, if she was being honest, did she have any desire to see a handful of her favorite people gaoled or hanged in public squares because she'd written a front-page article that exposed them.

Becoming a respected journalist had been her ambition for her entire adult life, yet she was just now starting to understand what that would mean. If she was forced to choose between the man she loved and realizing her one chance at a story of a lifetime...

"You're old," she said to her father.

He stopped speaking mid-word, eyes wide. "What?"

"You're in pain," she continued. He had told her. She hadn't listened. "You can't sleep, you can't walk, you want to retire. You're right. Let's do it."

His mouth fell open. "Now?"

"Yes, now." She leapt to her feet and retrieved the bucket of type in order to return the rest of her neatly ordered design to the chaotic pile. Her muscles rebelled, but she battered through her grief. "Why stop on Tuesday, when we can stop today?"

She wouldn't even mind being maid-of-all-work again. Endless, back-breaking chores would give her something to do besides sit around feeling empty.

Father grabbed the bucket from her hands and jerked it out of her reach.

"We have a duty to print." His eyes shone with zeal. "This is the big Yuletide issue, and the time of year when our community needs us most. People are counting on the Gazette. Our subscribers expect it, and Cressmouth expects it. We'll announce our retirement on the back page."

"I'll send a note," she said quickly. "Hand-written. To everyone on our list. Here are the dates on the bill at the winter theatre, here are the prices for sleigh rides, by the way you won't be hearing from us again. We can even re-run last year's edition, just like you suggested."

He wouldn't really ruin the le Ducs' lives, would he? Not when he could see how much it meant to her. How much *Bastien* meant.

His implacable tone bristled with superiority. "In addition to our community, we also have a duty to our countrymen. I was right never to trust the le Ducs. They're criminals. And criminals should go to prison."

"No," she whispered. "I can't."

"I'm proud of you," he continued as if she hadn't spoken, beaming at her in a way that he hadn't since before her mother had fallen ill. "I thought your interest in journalism was a passing phase. I didn't believe women were even capable of the sort of probing, investigative truth-finding required. After all, you were the trusting miss who invited the scoundrel who..."

Eve's stomach twisted.

Father curled his lip. "Once our more important subscribers read your article, you'll have the recognition for 'real journalism' you've always craved. Maybe you *will* end up in London, after all."

Her heart leapt at his prediction, causing her shoulders to crumple in shame. Weren't those the words she'd been longing to hear? The exact future she'd been working toward? All she had to do to earn the respect of fellow journalists was destroy the family of the man she loved.

Guilt and horror soured her stomach. All she'd wanted was to prove herself, to help Bastien, and instead she'd endangered his entire family. Once again, she'd trusted the wrong man. This time, it was her father. She would not allow him to ruin lives.

"No," she said again, her voice stronger this time. "I won't let you do it. I love him."

Father recoiled, his fleeting respect instantly replaced by years of betrayal and distrust.

"It doesn't matter," he said flatly. "Rules are rules. Laws are more important than love."

"Where does it end?" she asked. "They smuggle illegal shipments, but they don't drink it all themselves. Am I also supposed to print the names of every squire and aristocrat who enjoys the occasional glass of brandy?"

"If you *know* their names," Father said coldly, "then yes."

"That's half of England." Her voice rose. "Many of whom are good people!"

"And perhaps they wouldn't have been swayed to evil if men like the le Ducs weren't dangling temptation in front of their noses." His gaze turned calculating. "This is our opportunity to get rid of them."

"What about Jack?" she pointed out desperately. "You like him. He's English, he's a good father, he's been our neighbor for decades. You can't just implicate the le Ducs. Jack's family will go down with the same ship."

"Then he shouldn't have allowed their

poison to enter his life." Father began filling the empty space with new type. He was going to write this article with or without her. "This is our last issue, Eve. We're going to go out with a bang."

CHAPTER 15

Eve thumped on Bastien's front door.

It was past dawn; the smithy should be open. It was not. Cold and silent, it seemed as empty as this cottage. She knocked harder.

Delighted, Duenna added her voice to the mix.

Father's walking-stick slowed him down, but temper alone ensured he'd be right on Eve's heels in just a few minutes. She needed to talk to Bastien.

The door swung open.

She nearly sagged in relief. "Bastien!"

But it was not Bastien. It was a harried-looking footman.

She ran past him. She did not need directions to Bastien's bedchamber.

He was on his knees in front of a leather trunk, laying perfectly folded shirts and waistcoats in neat stacks. He leapt to his feet in surprise when he saw her.

Not the good kind of surprise. The *I-wish-you-hadn't-come* kind.

"What are you doing?" she blurted.

"Packing," he replied evenly. "What are *you* doing here?"

But her brain was too jumbled with the scene in front of her to remember any of the careful speech she'd constructed while racing to his door.

"Why are you packing?" She stepped forward uncertainly. "I didn't think you were leaving until after Twelfth Night. Epiphany, you said."

"And I didn't think you were planning to send myself, my brother, and my best friend to the gallows in order to increase the prestige of your quarterly gazette." He lifted his palms. "Yet here we are."

She straightened her shoulders and met his gaze straight on. "I'm not going to do it."

"*I* am," came her father's voice right behind her.

"Thank you so much for dropping by to clarify authorship." Sarcasm dripped from

Bastien's words. "That question would have kept me up all night."

Eve whirled to face her father. "You are *not* going to print a single word."

"It's my paper," he reminded her. "And my printing press."

"I know a man with a smithy," she shot back. "He'll loan me a hammer."

"Rules are rules, Eve." God, how she hated that phrase. Father shook his walking-stick toward Bastien. "When criminals break laws, there are repercussions. I need only pen a letter to the closest MP, and—"

"—and it'll be your word against mine." Eve's voice was as hard as her resolve. Father would no longer wrest control of her life from her. Nor would she allow him to destroy anyone else's out of misplaced superiority.

Bastien did not look convinced.

She turned to her father and crossed her arms. "What proof do you have that anything untoward has occurred?"

He pointed his finger. "Sébastien le Duc is packing a suitcase right before my eyes, ready to scurry away from justice like the rat that he—"

"He's *packing*. Most people who are going on a journey pack luggage to take with them.

He and his brother have made no secret of their desire to go home to France. Since they don't intend to return here, wouldn't it be far stranger if they were not taking care to prepare their belongings accordingly?"

Father stared at her. "But you said—"

"—that their smithy was the heart of Cressmouth. You destroyed my type, but I still have the handwritten original. If we print the Gazette, it will be with that article on the front page."

Bastien's brow furrowed. "*If* you print the Gazette?"

"Father wishes to retire and sell the machine for parts. If my proposal does not meet his approval, I have encouraged him to retire posthaste. Indeed, *you* own a smithy. Would you be interested in purchasing bits of secondhand iron to smelt down in your forge?"

His confusion did not lift. "But... you wanted..."

"I *did* want," she admitted. "Ambition gave me a reason to live, when I needed it most. I love to write. I wanted to use that talent to build others up, not tear people down."

Father leaned on his cane, his eyes angry. "If you don't run that story, there's no glory for you. No recognition as a respected journalist. Those papers you dreamed of working at will never know your name at all."

"True," she said quietly. "Words have power. And mercy is just as potent as destruction."

She turned to Bastien.

He visibly tensed.

She deserved that.

Eve let out a deep breath. "When I trusted the wrong person, I lost more than my mother. I lost my father's respect. And I lost my faith in myself. Over the years, I also lost sight of the most important truth of all: Nobody's perfect. Not you, not me, not even Father, though he'll never admit it."

Bastien's dark gaze was indecipherable.

Father's empurpled countenance, less so.

"You can't ignore blatant disrespect of our government and our laws when it's happening right under your nose," he spluttered.

"It won't be." She gestured at the trunk. "He's leaving." She lifted her eyes to Bastien. "And if he can still tolerate my company, I'll sail off with him."

Bastien froze, his gaze still and bright, his thoughts unfathomable.

"F-fine." Father's face was ashen, as though he'd just now realized he should take his daughter's feelings seriously. "We won't print the article. But if you think I'm inviting a known blackguard into my life…"

"I'm not inviting him into your life." She turned back to Bastien. "I'm inviting him into mine."

His brown eyes searched hers. "You'd walk away from everything you know and love… just to be with *me?*"

"I don't want to leave Cressmouth," she admitted. "But I don't want to lose you more. I love you, Bastien le Duc."

His mouth parted, but no sound came out.

Her cheeks burned. "I was consumed with 'investigating' others so that I wouldn't have time to examine myself. I've always known you planned to leave. I never guessed you'd be taking my heart with you. I couldn't let you walk away without knowing the whole truth. In case you didn't hear it, I'll say it again: I love you. No matter what."

There. The words were out, and words had power. But would they be powerful enough?

Or was it too late?

CHAPTER 16

She loved him.

Bastien stared at Eve's upturned green eyes, shining at him with a mix of both hope and resignation.

She loved him, was prepared to defy her father and overlook a few hundred counts of tax evasion and illegal transportation, was even willing to step on a boat and say goodbye to everything she held dear…

And she didn't even realize *he* loved *her*?

Before he could set the record straight, Lucien stepped into the bedchamber behind Eve's father.

Just what the situation needed: more spectators. Every muscle in Bastien's body tensed.

"Grand frère…" He pointed toward the corridor. *"Out."*

Lucien stepped further inside. "I've been listening since they arrived, but I can't see faces from the hallway."

"This is England." Mr. Shelling's face grew mottled. "Speak English."

"This is their house," Eve hissed back. "Do you want them to come tell you what to do in yours?"

"Oh, very well." Lucien let out a long-suffering sigh. "I like her."

Bastien ignored him and turned to Eve.

"Last night, I received the passage to France I'd sent away for." He cleared his throat. "Do you know what my first thought was when I saw those tickets?"

She tilted her head and frowned. "'I hope I don't lose these?'"

"*My* first thought," Lucien agreed, and patted the breast-pocket where he'd sequestered the tickets.

"'I can't walk away from Eve,'" Bastien corrected softly. "Those tickets had once symbolized escape and freedom and finally going home. Now they felt like the opposite. Running away from what I truly desired, launching myself further from my true home. The freedom I needed most was the freedom to choose what I really wanted."

Her empathy was palpable. "I've spent my life yearning for that freedom."

"I've spent my life waiting for you," Bastien said. There was no point in making her wait longer to hear the words. He intended to tell her over and over again for the rest of their lives. "I love you, Eve Shelling. I love your village. I love your dog, even though she knocked me into a puddle while I was wearing my favorite waistcoat—"

"Not the one with blue-and-green spangles," Lucien whispered in faux horror.

Bastien carried on. "I know what it's like to lose one's home. I would never inflict that on someone else. Nor would I ever ask someone I cared about to give up their aspirations."

"Don't write about us, though," Lucien muttered.

Bastien sent him a glare. "She's not going to write *bad* things."

"Tell her to find a new aspiration," Lucien insisted. "Tell her that being a 'real' reporter isn't as elegant as she thinks. Tell her that if she was a journalist in London right now, she'd be writing about the Tottenham Court Road beer flood whilst standing knee-deep in fermented porter."

"Shut *up*, Lucien." Bastien paused. "Wait. You've been reading the newspapers?"

"Slowly," his brother admitted, self-conscious. "I'm tired of the children's books in the castle circulating library. I have *The History of Little Goody Two-Shoes* memorized. Please don't tell anyone."

"We'll talk later." Bastien turned and took Eve's hands in his. "I can't promise you a better life than the one you have right now. All I can promise is to be *in* it, from this day forward, come what may."

"Except gallows," Lucien put in. "That would stop things."

Bastien sent him a quelling look over one shoulder.

Lucien held up his hands. "If I had the money, I'd buy the printing press from her father and give it to Eve."

Bastien arched his brows. "I thought you planned to take every possible penny to France."

"Are we both still going to France?" Lucien countered. "It sounds like you want to stay."

Bastien *did* want to stay. That *was* what he was suggesting.

But where did that leave Lucien? Bastien

couldn't keep smuggling, which meant his only income would be the smithy. If he didn't sell, there'd be no buyer. No buyer, no money. No way for Lucien to support himself in France.

Bastien couldn't ask Eve to give up her dreams, but he would never force his brother to do so, either.

It was an impasse.

"What's wrong?" Her hands trembled in his, the fingers suddenly cold. "It's not possible, is it?"

"We'll make it possible," he said quickly. "*I'll* make it possible."

"Bastien... can solve... anything," Lucien added in thickly accented English.

Eve and her father's jaws fell open with perfect synchronicity.

Lucien gazed back at them smugly.

"I've got it." Bastien's blood raced with excitement.

Lucien blinked.

"*Très vite.*" That was fast. "Even for you."

Bastien shook his head. "The answer was here all along. I didn't see it because we weren't looking for ways to stay." He switched to English. "The Harpers made an offer for the smithy."

Eve gasped. "That's…" Indecision flickered across her face. "Is it wonderful or terrible?"

"The best news in the world," he assured her. "They're willing to pay handsomely for the smithy, but they don't have a blacksmith to run it. Lucien will be off in France spending their coin, but I'll be right here on the farm. They'd have to pay me, of course, to keep managing things until they can find someone to replace me…"

Eve's eyes twinkled. "No one could ever replace you. I'm pretty sure a front-page article to that effect will be published in this month's edition of the Cressmouth Gazette. The Harpers will simply have to keep paying you until you voluntarily choose to retire."

Mr. Shelling let out a long-suffering sigh, and turned to Bastien. "You should think about raising your salary."

All three of them whirled to face him.

He leaned on his walking-stick. "If I'm to be saddled with one of you, I want to be certain you can take care of my daughter. Then again, I don't know that I *am* landed with you. Is there a question you've been meaning to ask me?"

"With all due respect, sir…" Bastien looked him in the eye without blinking. "The lady clearly stated that *she* would like to be the one making decisions about her life." He dropped to one knee and lifted Eve's fingers to his chest. "My dearest love, with every beat of my unabashedly French heart, it is you and you alone who—"

"*Yes*," she blurted, and launched herself into his arms.

Lucien placed his hands to his throat. "Quick, *papa*, write to the nearest MP. Your child is wrinkling Bastien's waistcoat!"

Bastien was too busy kissing his betrothed to dignify his brother's comments with an answer.

Besides, if the root cause of a man's disheveled apparel was going to be because he'd been passionately embracing his bride-to-be...

He rather thought he was starting to *like* wrinkles.

24 December, 1814

In the end, Lucien le Duc didn't have to purchase the printing press after all in order to give Eve unfettered access to it.

Mr. Thompson, Marlowe Castle's solicitor and manager, acquired the press and all its accoutrements for the castle trust, and employed Eve as editor-in-chief of the now *monthly* Cressmouth Gazette.

The charts of sleigh ride prices and the theatre schedule were still there, along with plenty of cheerful froth about wassail recipes, carol lyrics, the proper tending of a Yule log, and how to decorate one of the local ever-greens like Queen Charlotte had done with a yew tree.

But that was only half of the content. Eve now had a team of independent journalists who submitted articles on all aspects of Cressmouth life and news. There were advice columns, birth and wedding columns, a farmer's almanac, local advertisements… and, of course, the esteemed honor of Resident of the Month, written by Eve herself.

To her surprise and gratification, there was no need to move to London and become a faceless contributor to an unwieldy daily paper in order to be respected. There was no shame in staying local and supporting her community. Cressmouth was her home, and they needed her here.

Besides, working for the castle trust af-forded her far more freedoms—and a much larger salary—than she would have ever found elsewhere.

Instead of being an overlooked junior con-tributor submitting uncredited article after uncredited article due to her gender and lim-ited experience, she was the one everyone came to with their questions and ideas.

Together, they could make the Gazette the

official voice of Cressmouth. They could tell *all* its stories, and present their village and themselves to the world as the wonderful, complex, tightly-knit family they were.

"Are you certain it's not nepotism to choose your betrothed as the first official Resident of the Month?" Bastien asked.

She grinned and curled into him on the chaise before the fire. "It's definitely nepotism. I have no regrets. Besides, you're not my 'betrothed' anymore."

"Mm, that's right." He flipped her onto her back and covered her body with his. "Now that we're husband and wife, does that mean we need not concern ourselves with propriety anymore?"

"What in the dickens is 'propriety?'" She slid her fingers into his hair and pulled him to her.

"Wait," he murmured between kisses. "It's Christmas Eve. Don't you want your present?"

She gave him a wicked grin. "Tonight and every night."

But the truth was, they'd already been given the best gift they could ever ask for:

Each other.

~

What will happen when "deliciously brooding" Lucien le Duc clashes with the irreverent and indomitable Miss Margaret Church?

Join the fun in *The Duke's Desire,* the next romance in the *12 Dukes of Christmas* series!

ACKNOWLEDGMENTS

As always, I could not have written this book without the invaluable support of my beta readers and editors. Huge thanks go out to Erica Monroe and Tessa Shapcott. You are the best!

Lastly, I want to thank the *12 Dukes of Christmas* facebook group, my *Historical Romance Book Club,* and my fabulous street team. Your enthusiasm makes the romance happen.

Thank you so much!

Love talking books with fellow readers?

Join the ***Historical Romance Book Club*** for prizes, books, and live chats with your favorite romance authors:
Facebook.com/groups/HistRomBookClub

Check out the ***12 Dukes of Christmas*** facebook group for giveaways and exclusive content:
Facebook.com/groups/DukesOfChristmas

Join the ***Rogues to Riches*** facebook group for insider info and first looks at future books in the series:

Facebook.com/groups/RoguesToRiches

Check out the **Dukes of War** facebook group for giveaways and exclusive content:
Facebook.com/groups/DukesOfWar

And check out the official website for sneak peeks and more:
www.EricaRidley.com/books

THE DUKE'S DESIRE

Margaret Church adores two things: life in a village of perennial Yuletide, and the freedoms of being a spinster with no reputation to protect. Oh, very well, *three* things: She's harbored a secret *tendre* for Christmas curmudgeon Lucien le Duc since the moment she first glimpsed him. But the sexy blacksmith won't give her the time of day, much less a night of torrid passion.

Ever since Lucien le Duc was forced to flee his beloved France during the revolution, his all-consuming goal has been to recover not only his lost land and fortune, but also his rightful place among the French aristocracy. He would *never* be distracted by an English dairy maid's sultry glances... or her soul-consuming kisses… or the temptation to turn one night into forever…

The *12 Dukes of Christmas* is a series of heartwarming Regency romps nestled in a picturesque snow-covered village. Twelve delightful romances… and plenty of delicious dukes!

ABOUT THE AUTHOR

Erica Ridley is a *New York Times* and *USA Today* best-selling author of historical romance novels.

In the new *12 Dukes of Christmas* series, enjoy witty, heartwarming Regency romps nestled in a picturesque snow-covered village. After all, nothing heats up a winter night quite like finding oneself in the arms of a duke!

Her two most popular series, the *Dukes of War* and *Rogues to Riches*, feature roguish peers and dashing war heroes who find love amongst the splendor and madness of Regency England.

When not reading or writing romances, Erica can be found riding camels in Africa, zip-lining through rainforests in Central America, or getting hopelessly lost in the middle of Budapest.